BERLIN-WARSZAWA EXPRESS

EAMON McGRATH

ECW Press / a misFit book

This is a work of fiction. Names, characters, places, and incidents either are the product of the author's imagination or are used fictitiously, and any resemblance to actual persons, living or dead, business establishments, events, or locales is entirely coincidental.

Editor for the press: Michael Holmes / a misFit book
Cover design: Natalie Olsen / kisscut design
MISFIT   Author photo: Peter Dreimanis
Cover photo: © Image Source / Getty Images International

Published by ECW Press
665 Gerrard Street East
Toronto, Ontario, Canada M4M 1Y2
416-694-3348 / info@ecwpress.com

LIBRARY AND ARCHIVES CANADA
CATALOGUING IN PUBLICATION

McGrath, Eamon, author
Berlin-Warszawa express /
Eamon McGrath.

Issued in print and electronic formats.
ISBN 978-1-77041-328-3 (paperback)
ALSO ISSUED AS: 978-1-77305-027-0 (PDF)
978-1-77305-026-3 (EPUB)

I. TITLE.

PS8625.G72B47 2017   C813'.6
C2016-906407-7   C2016-906408-5

The publication of *Berlin-Warszawa Express* has been generously supported by the Canada Council for the Arts, which last year invested $153 million to bring the arts to Canadians throughout the country, and by the Government of Canada through the Canada Book Fund. *Nous remercions le Conseil des arts du Canada de son soutien. L'an dernier, le Conseil a investi 153 millions de dollars pour mettre de l'art dans la vie des Canadiennes et des Canadiens de tout le pays. Ce livre est financé en partie par le gouvernement du Canada.* We also acknowledge the support of the Ontario Arts Council (OAC), an agency of the Government of Ontario, which last year funded 1,737 individual artists and 1,095 organizations in 223 communities across Ontario for a total of $52.1 million, and the contribution of the Government of Ontario through the Ontario Book Publishing Tax Credit and the Ontario Media Development Corporation.

PRINTED AND BOUND IN CANADA   PRINTING: COACH HOUSE   5 4 3 2 1

TO MAGGIE, FOR PUTTING UP WITH
ME BEING GONE ALL THE TIME.

AND TO MY MOM WENDY,
FOR INTRODUCING ME TO ALL THE
MADNESS OF ART IN THE FIRST PLACE.

I'm in Paris. I'm sitting, elbows on the bar, a pint in my outstretched hand. Pigeons are racing outside, and the hum of Paris traffic in the distance can be heard from the end of the street. I am not at home. I have stepped through the tunnel and gone to the other side as if through a magical wardrobe or down the rabbit hole. I'm on the road.

I'd spent the night before in a dingy Paris rehearsal space in a suburb called Pantin. Up the stairs and outside, there were drunken homeless men reclining against a tall brick wall opposite a group of orphaned Algerian children playing football in the street.

Fuelled by beer, scotch, and hash, and the sound of the mind breaking down its doors, I played music long into the morning with some newfound Parisian friends. From that place underground, I realized it had taken me what felt like years of coming to Paris to feel like I'd finally connected to it: there's so much power and soul and mayhem and virtue here, though most of it lies hidden away, like rats in the sewer. I felt like I'd finally discovered the true heartbeat of the French capital. The Paris beneath Paris, beneath Paris, beneath. Friendship through the blood of music.

The next afternoon, at a café, I was meeting Fangs, an old friend of mine. I closed my eyes and rubbed them in circles, trying to shake off the night before and prepare myself for our conversation. I downed a beer, ordered another, and Fangs walked in.

"Holy shit. It's been a long time."

I used to write for Fangs back in Edmonton, before I'd gone and surrendered my life to the road. He was an editor at the local music paper but had moved on to a bigger city, better things. Fangs used to sneak me into bars when I was underage, to review bands for him, and slip me pints of beer like I was Cameron Crowe in a prairie remake of *Almost Famous*. Before he'd even sat down, the arguments about music began like no time had passed at all.

"I hate the Dirty Projectors. Bullshit Brooklyn spoiled-white-kid afrobeat wannabe crap."

"The vocal harmonies, though. C'mon and be a man about it. What do you think of the War on Drugs?"

"Best recording band right now. Stole the torch from the Drones post *Gala Mill*."

"I saw the first Murder City Devils reunion show. Was great. The follow-ups were tragic."

"Should've been at the Replacements reunion. No bands do that anymore."

"*Alien Lanes, Alien Lanes, Alien Lanes. Bee Thousand* is true Pollard. It's got 'Tractor Rape Chain' for Christ's sake."

It went on like that for hours: two writers yelling at the top of their lungs with beer falling down their throats until grammar and punctuation were lost. Claude Mysterieux, the bartender, circled around the café with *Exile on Main Street* blaring from the speakers. He closed the shutters down and lit a cigarette.

"*Madames et monsieurs*, it's that time," he said, waving his hands. "We have hidden from the authorities—smoke whatever you want in here."

When you measure the passing of time in kilometres or the number of shows you've played, it becomes viscous. You get trapped in it, a fleck of sand in sunscreen. Fangs and I were now immersed in this substance, sliding down the neck of the bottle together. I told Fangs that I was going to try to write a book. "But I'm trying to figure out how to start it. I just don't know how to start."

Fangs laughed the way a great editor does. "Start at the end."

That night Claude the bartender and I went back to his apartment with a bottle of Ballantine's and a can of soda, winding our way through the complex streets of Paris, along a canal in Oberkampf. While pissing in the water, Claude told me that in the summertime everybody dives in, and he's picked up tons of girls that way. The water moved slowly, a thick Parisian black: filth with an undisputed elegance to it. We stayed up all night drinking, and as I got my bag ready for the morning, we talked about the next round of shows. When I awoke, I headed to the Gare de Paris-Est and began my journey east to Berlin.

The first time I went to Berlin it was the middle of December, during what I would come to know as one of those dark, grey stretches of hibernation and north German solitude. It was in the middle of a tour that had begun in Holland and Belgium and woven its way through the streets of Paris, down to the south of Germany and into Switzerland, then carved a tunnel through the snow northeast along the Czech-Saxon border to the German capital, our easternmost destination.

There were five of us, including me alongside western Canada's legendary Stagger Tecumseh on bass,

Alberta expat Jack Valentine on keys, James Herbert Billiards behind the drum set, and guitarist and singer Ivan Reservoir. Doing two sets a night, we'd first act as Ivan's backing band, then climb back onstage and perform a set of my songs to headline the shows. When we drove into Berlin the sun was long down, and we found the venue in a storm of students crossing the street and drinking in pubs to hide from the cold. Immediately I knew this city went miles and miles deeper than it appeared to the naked eye, that underneath the concrete lurked something far more menacingly beautiful.

It was about seven o'clock when we entered the bar and introduced ourselves to the owner, a short and stocky Berliner named Pietr. This tour was ripe with overindulgence in the shadow of deep sadness: we were all strung out on booze and drugs, hopelessly broke and cold and miserable, driving through one of the worst European winters in recent memory, and Berlin itself was a slimy slew of snow. We were constantly in a cycle of coming down and getting high, and it was one of those tours where it seemed like every single night you met somebody who found a way of putting something up your nose. Pietr showed us our hostel room and explained the situation with the upstairs residents, how we had to play a subdued and quieter set because we weren't allowed to have a full drum kit in the bar—noise complaints had made loud punk rock impossible.

So we compromised with a suitcase kick drum and a towel over the snare, turned the amps down, dropped off our bags in the hostel after soundcheck, and poured some beers at the bar.

The scope and magnitude of the city began with the sight of the towering S-Bahn tracks, with all the people drinking on the street and in the bars, with all the lights and all the snow. Coupled with how little I knew about it at the time, not to mention how little sleep I was getting, I felt like I was in a little over my head.

After the show, Pietr was overjoyed: he'd loved the music and thought we played to the space perfectly. The songs came across, everyone in that little unlit backroom on some side street in Neukölln locked in a green applause. He took us over to the bar and gave us another round of fresh, cold beer.

"I'm really sick tonight," Pietr explained. "So, I'm sorry, I can't really drink with you, even after such a great show."

We told him it was fine and got to talking. Pietr told us about the city, about its life outside of everyone who visits, about how Berlin has always been a churning mass of culture, about how it's really this glowing, swirling, alien thing. One thing about Berlin that you learn before almost anything else is that Berliners love Berlin.

After a few more minutes, the conversation turned to the subject of German bitters. Someone said

Jägermeister and there was a tension in the conversation that you could have plucked like a guitar string.

"Jägermeister?" Pietr exclaimed. "Jägermeister tastes like the shit of a donkey!"

Either his sickness had subsided dramatically or his outrage had cured his exhaustion, because Pietr animatedly ordered us each three great German bitters, which came in shot glasses, full to the brim. James Billiards was off gallivanting with the women who existed on the edges of the night sky, and Ivan Reservoir had gone off to chase the future. Those still inside were thinking about the past.

It was just the three of us now: Stagger, Jack, and me. We consumed what felt like a gallon of alcohol between us in under three minutes. Stagger thanked Pietr and stepped outside after rolling his tobacco, and I joined him. Jack Valentine stayed inside, talking up a girl with the hope that maybe his pillow wouldn't be the window of the van.

"So should we go and see the Wall?" I asked as Stagger took a drag.

"Yeah, I think so. Seems like the appropriate thing." Stagger was up to his knees in a bank of wet snow. The whole sidewalk was covered in empty bottles and footprints that trudged through two feet of grey, sloshy stew. "Okay, we'll need a taxi to take us there. I have no idea where I'm going."

Feeling our thin blood finally make its way to our brains, we stepped back inside. Pietr was slumped against the wall in the corner, staring into space, his eyes dead from sickness and exhaustion, a thin line of drool dangling from his bottom lip to the floor.

"Don't worry about him," a regular said from down the bar. "He might not have shown it, but Pietr was trying to drink himself better hours ago, well before you guys showed up and did all those shots with him."

The girl Jack was talking to had vanished into the falling snow of the Berlin night. We convinced Jack to join us, and the three of us got into a cab and told the driver in extremely broken German where we wanted to go.

"The Wall," we said from the backseat. "Take us to the Wall."

"I don't know what you mean," he replied. "You want to go to the Wall? The Wall is in lots of places . . ."

"Take us to see a chunk of the Wall. It's our first time in Berlin."

His sly grin seemed to be hiding something when he said, "It's your first time here. Of course."

He stepped on the pedal and drove us through Neukölln and Kreuzberg, probably revelling in the fact that he could milk the last few bucks from the near-empty wallets of three Berlin first-timers. We tried to make conversation in a drunken soup of English, French, and German until, finally, he stopped the car and let us out.

I'm not sure how I imagined the tombstone to the end of the Cold War: a thick, invincible piece of rock, twenty feet high, racing through the middle of the city? Gun turrets, armoured cars, and then steel and stone covered in graffiti? Did it slice through the decaying urban landscape like a blade from the north to the south?

What I saw instead was a thin piece of chipped concrete that only stood about ten feet high. What was depicted throughout history as the greatest dividing line in the Western world seemed like a sheet of vandalized cardboard. I know now that we must have been at the East Side Gallery, a few football fields' worth of graffiti-covered Wall along the river Spree, on the border of Kreuzberg and Friedrichshain at the foot of the Oberbaumbrücke, but at the time it looked like this puny, unassuming joke. Right then, Berlin made so much more sense to me.

"This is the Wall?"

"Really?"

The taxi driver laughed, and we tried to figure out what all the fuss was about. Stupid kids, we realized that all that post-war tension was over something that didn't really stand so tall. Without the soldiers, without the guns, without the turrets, and without the Soviet Union, the Berlin Wall was just a canvas for kids with spray cans.

If you squint and imagine a Berlin Wall without

the armies that protected it, it doesn't seem so scary or important. Berliners had all their lives to learn that trick, and because of that, over time they'd learned that the Wall was more or less made of paper. That moment must have been when the city just walked right through it.

There was a kind of stillness in the December calm. The engine of the car was a faint hum over our drunken, astounded silence and the headlights illuminated the gently falling snow. We felt like we'd crossed this rite of passage, our heads tipped back as we gazed up at the Wall. The driver still snickered at us, basking in the warmth of his heated car. In that moment, our hardships seemed endurable, comical even. All of us forgot where we were going, and where we had come from. We sighed and got back in the taxi and I drifted off into the dark realms of a dreamless night, my mind painted a solid black with the powerful palette of alcohol.

Disaster followed disaster on that tour. The day before we left I fell off a roof and lost some teeth. Ivan Reservoir, the morning after a Belgian beer and amphetamine frenzy, ran headlong into the thick black Belgian woods. A rolled-over semi truck stranded us motionless for fifteen hours on the autobahn between Freiburg and Frankfurt, so we polished off a case of Beck's and slept in the van, in total gridlock in the snow. We cancelled a show in Switzerland because the mountain passes were closed and we would have been stuck there over the whole of Christmastime. The tour ended with us having to sleep on the floor of Heathrow for five days and four nights because of grounded planes. All of us were broke. It was not a happy time.

First, my teeth. It was after a long day of rehearsing. Stagger and I were sitting on the roof of my girlfriend's apartment at Bloor and Ossington, staring out through the dark black night at the Toronto skyline, a massive, sprawling entity full of red and blue beckoning lights.

It was raining and we were drunk. The rain began light and easy and then it started pounding down. We kept laughing and talking about me leaving Edmonton—I'd only been living in the Big Smoke for five or six months at that point—and about touring across Canada. We talked about driving through the Rockies in snowstorms and about soldiering through the rainy muck of the Maritimes to make it to Halifax in time for soundcheck.

We talked about going overseas and hitting the road and how excited we were for a new frontier, away from the Canadian Prairies, which was the only home we'd ever shared. There was a great sense of optimism in our young minds. The band was sounding good. We were all excited and looking forward to the future and to new horizons, to that place where the highway disappears into something bookmark-thin, an otherworldly place where the signposts are written in words from a mysterious, unreadable language.

It was about then I got the great idea to scale down the sloping roof and climb into my girlfriend's window, a young and stupid Cyrano de Bergerac hoping to romantically coax her to come outside in the pouring rain and drink with us.

"It's okay, Stag," I said. "I've done this tons of times."

She wasn't waking up, although I was banging louder and louder on the window, so I decided to leave it alone and climb back up. As I did, my foot hydroplaned from under me and I started to fall.

Somehow I had the wherewithal to grab a telephone line that dangled across the roof and I swung into the side of the wall. I smashed my face against the building and it was like a searing blast of impossible pain. I could feel my wrist extend, and I landed on my back on the balcony that stretched out beneath her window, at least another two storeys down. Stagger yelled and ran to the side of the roof. I lay there for a moment, soaking wet, as the rain just kept falling.

"Help," I shouted, moving my arms and legs to make sure nothing was broken. It was my mouth and face that hurt the most. I kept yelling. "It's my teeth . . . my teeth are *dust* . . ."

My tongue felt around my mouth and I noticed that everything was chipped and mangled. Two teeth wiggled around in my jaw. Throbbing pain surged through me with every heartbeat. I stumbled to my feet, knocked on my girlfriend's roommate's window, woke her up, pissed her off, went up the stairs to my girlfriend's room, and passed out on the bed in a torrent of madness. When I awoke in the morning, there was a halo of blood on the pillow.

"Why the *fuck* didn't you go to the hospital?" she said to me, wiping blood off my face with a damp rag. She shone a flashlight in my eyes to see if I had a concussion. "You're such an idiot. What the *fuck* were you thinking? What the *fuck* were you doing?"

I told her I was drunk, just trying to be romantic, just trying to be funny. I didn't go to the hospital because I felt all right. I was, however, worried about the loose, punishingly sore teeth. I had to go to a dentist, immediately. Things felt dislodged and out of place. I felt crooked and out of order. And I was to leave that night for Europe.

Valentine went to the dentist with me and sat in the waiting room as I lay in the chair waiting for an answer. The X-rays came back and my teeth had completely shattered, still lodged by the root in my gums, ready to fall out any second. The dentist was shocked that I wasn't in even more pain, and I told him that I was catching a plane in under eight hours, so he took me upstairs and yanked the bastards out.

I came out to the waiting room, tears welling in my eyes and blood pouring into the gauze stuffed in my mouth. Valentine stared at me and I stood as pale as a ghost. I'd lost something I was never going to get back.

"Jesus," he said. "Are you going to be okay?"

"Yeah," I replied, unsure. "I guess."

I took some painkillers, packed my stuff, said goodbye, and we got on the subway headed for the airport.

Then there was the bump of speed that sat quietly on the key in my outstretched hand, pointed toward Stagger's nose, as he was behind the wheel. He had slept the night before and so had all five working senses while the rest of us had stayed up all night drunk and high as shit and arguing to the point where the band was breaking up and we thought we weren't friends anymore.

There was no turning back from that kind of evening. Relationships are beyond repair when you say the kinds of things we said to each other that night. All rational thought was missing in action and our emotions were the soldiers left holding the rifles. Lashing out, lashing in, nothing was sacred. With every line of speed and shot of whiskey we punished each other, and ourselves, for what we'd put each other through.

As the sun rose, we realized that it was time to leave for Groningen and Stagger was the only one fit to drive, even though he couldn't drive stick. As he sipped his coffee behind the wheel, he tried not to stall as he motioned with smiling eyes at the little bag I'd taken out of my coat pocket. We both laughed, he cranked Motörhead, and I spooned some speed on the end of my house key. There was only madness now.

I saw Ivan's eyes open in the rear-view mirror as he caught a glimpse of Stagger snorting what was perched on the end of my key and lost it.

"That's *it*. Pull the van over," he said, the volume in his voice increasing. "*Pull the fucking van over now.*"

As we pulled to the side of the Belgian highway, hazards blinking furiously, Reservoir leapt out of the side door and bolted like a fork of lightning into the northern forest. He had the clothes on his back, his laptop bag in his right hand, and the toque on his head. He was psychotic with exhaustion, coming down, perpetually hungover, and completely lost at sea.

Jack Valentine, just as high as we were, looked at us with wide, condemning eyes. "What the *fuck*, you guys?!"

"Let him go, I'm not stopping him," I said, twist-tying the bag shut.

Stagger laughed. "Me neither."

Valentine burst out of the car, ran after Reservoir, and, with the energy of all those amphetamines in the stride of his sprint, finally caught up with him.

From the side-view mirrors, we could see the weary and exhausted figures yelling at each other, two small black dots against the sun low in the sky, the backdrop of the Benelux highway and black woods behind them. Everything had totally collapsed. Disaster after disaster.

The argument I imagined them having might as well have been real.

Reservoir: "I'm getting on the first flight outta here. I'm going *home*. I can't fucking take this anymore."

Valentine's response came out of his mouth like a comic-book balloon, lost like us in the middle of nowhere. "How are you going to get a flight out of here, exactly? Where are you gonna go, Frankfurt? Schiphol? Brussels? How are you going to get there? How the fuck are you going to get to Frankfurt?"

"I'll . . . hitchhike." The highway traffic sped by. "I'll get to the airport, I'll get on the next flight home to Toronto . . ."

"No one is going to stop for you. No one will pick *you* up. We're going to this show. Drink some water, get yourself together, and let's get outta here."

"No, I can't, I . . ."

Stagger and I sat in the front seat of the van, shaking our heads and laughing. Everything except the van had broken down.

"Is it kickin' in yet?" I said to him with a grin, Lemmy screaming through the small, tinny, blownout speakers.

"Not really," he said, "to be honest. Not really sure

what all this fuckin' fuss is about. I'm *still* better off to drive than anyone else here."

After what seemed like hours, Valentine finally coaxed Reservoir back into his place in the van.

"I'm *not* cool with the driver doing speed behind the wheel," Reservoir said.

"Yeah sure, man, whatever, sorry," Stagger replied. "But you're not going home. There's no way outta this. So buckle up."

I turned Lemmy back up and we kept heading north.

A few nights after that, there was the gridlocked madness of getting stranded on the autobahn.

"Why the fuck are we stopping?" somebody said, can't remember who, as we ground to a halt on the highway, the snow pummelling us from all directions. We'd gone from well over one hundred and twenty clicks to not moving at all. I reached into the back and opened a Beck's from the case we'd taken from the last venue.

Like a common cold, the contagious sound of a cracking beer cap echoed and within a few hours everyone—except Reservoir, the driver—was well on their way to being completely wasted.

"So what's going on, anyways?" I asked him, after getting out to piss.

"I think it's an accident," he said, "and what the fuck? Are you guys actually all drunk on me, already?"

"Come on, man, what else are we gonna do?" I replied. "Besides, it's been like four hours!"

By that time, we'd missed our soundcheck and it was looking like there was no hope for our show. We'd called the venue and things were not sitting well. Another two or three hours passed. There was more fighting, can't remember about what, and the snow continued to fall outside. I passed out for a while.

I awoke with a jerk as the van was moving forward. Everyone else was now unconscious, except for Ivan Reservoir, still behind the wheel.

"Jesus Christ," I said, rubbing the sleep from my eyes. "How long was I out?"

"About five hours," he spat, pissed off. "I've been sitting here alone and awake for *five hours*, man."

"Fuck," I said. "I'm so sorry."

As we moved forward, inching along the autobahn, we passed an eighteen-wheeler completely rolled over, hiding behind what looked like solid walls of snow. Someone had extinguished a fire. There were three cars, in pieces, surrounding it. Nothing was left of the driver's cabin, the windshield was crumpled, a door was off its hinges.

Reservoir had a thousand-yard stare and we both sat speechless as the wheels slowly turned. I looked out the passenger side window at the accident, the sound of three sleeping bodies conducting the steady rhythm of the van driving forward through the night.

The tour ended in Switzerland. It was about eight p.m. in Winterthur, and we had two shows to go. We'd loaded into the bar, soundchecked, and were eating dinner with the promoter as we brought up the weather report.

There was a monumental storm headed our way, through Germany and down into Switzerland, and planes were being grounded on runways all across the continent. We had tonight in Winterthur, and then the following evening down south in Locarno, and then we faced an eighteen-hour drive to London after the show before flying home.

The weather had been getting worse all week. Highway traffic was always gridlocked, and the trips across Switzerland were getting longer because of the near-standstills on the mountain passes through the Alps. The can of worms had opened. Should we cancel tomorrow night? Otherwise, it looked like we weren't going home for Christmas.

"I've never cancelled a show," Reservoir said. "I just don't feel right about this. We should take our chances and head there. Finish the tour properly, on a good note."

"Man, I've never cancelled a show either," I said. "But let's look at the facts. Think about what we've *been* through. We don't need this."

The promoter sat, pensive at his computer, and exhaled cigarette smoke. "Well," he said. "It seems you guys have to make a choice."

After another hour of arguing over beers, Stagger and Billiards left to go outside to smoke, and Valentine, Reservoir, and I stayed inside to make a decision. After another fifteen minutes, tonight in Winterthur was going to be our final show.

After that, you can only admit defeat. Disaster, after disaster, after disaster. With all of the fighting, arguing, resentment, and now this cancellation: it felt like it had all been for nothing. In a moment like that, you get swallowed by solemnity. Reservoir got up from the table and went outside. Valentine waited for a few more minutes and did the same. I stayed at the table, smoking, staring into my drink.

The promoter got up to use the bathroom, and as I went to refill my glass, I caught a glimpse of an email on his screen from the Locarno promoter, after he'd sent them the news. I clenched my fists when I read the message: "These guys are fucking crazy."

I took my beer out into the snow and walked around outside in the cold for a while. We all reconvened at the venue and played our last show of the tour, which was cut short because of sound restrictions, and everyone looked pale, as though they were going to cry. We went to another bar after the set, and Reservoir spent the last of the band fund on one round of shots and beers. We had nothing. We'd officially lost it all.

The next morning, we got up at eight and headed straight out of Switzerland. We didn't get to London till midnight. Gridlocked highways, French toll roads, delays on boarding the Calais–Dover ferry, and a general feeling of defeat stretched the trip to a sixteen-hour ordeal. There was no way we would've gotten to London on time had we played Locarno.

Relieved, we dropped off the van, dropped off the gear, and got in a minicab to Heathrow with a small window of time left to catch our flights that took off at midnight. But immediately upon arrival we knew something was wrong.

The airport was bedlam and panic: pallets of bottled water had been forklifted at random places on the floor. Lineups around the baggage drop-off desks stretched for miles. There were people shivering underneath silver blankets that had been supplied by the Salvation Army. It was like a disaster film.

"What the fuck is going on?" Reservoir asked a British Airways worker.

"Heathrow is closed, mate," he replied. "Nothing is taking off. All the planes have been grounded."

Fuck it, I thought. We cracked a bottle of liquor that we'd snuck through the border and started pounding it. We gathered pieces of cardboard, plastic, and velvet rope dividers and, bit by bit, built us a fort, the way you did when you were at home, a young kid in the summer. We unrolled our sleeping bags beneath the cardboard and plastic roof, laughing our asses off, shots of vodka carrying us off to a better place and time, our last chance for happiness.

Valentine went off to the bathroom and a few minutes later I followed, really having to piss. I saw him standing over a sink, flossing, and what looked like pints of blood gushing out his mouth and circling down the drain. His red, drunken eyes looked at me through the mirror, and my eyebrows rose in disbelief.

"Looks like you're not the only one losing your teeth."

From his spitting out the massive amounts of blood that were forming in his gums, the sink was a deep, bloody crimson, and the blood wasn't slowing.

I left the bathroom and rejoined James, Ivan, and Stag, still howling and laughing together under the fort. For a tiny second I imagined that the fort wasn't made of garbage and airport benches and discarded trash, but something from a better, sunnier time, and then we all descended into sleep.

We woke in the morning to airport security ripping apart our makeshift hideaway. They took the velvet rope dividers and walked all over our sleeping bags, stomping and swearing, frantically setting up queues around the check-in counters, crushing our ditched effort for joy.

"Come on," I said, still drunk. "Give us a break, what the fuck . . ."

"*Up*," they kept repeating. "*Up.*"

We spent the next four days and five nights on

the floor of that airport. You couldn't leave in case your flight was called, in case the BAA decided to let planes take off, and if you weren't there to jump in the queue, then there was no telling how much longer you'd have to wait before you were called again. So we waited.

"Give us shovels," I remember the Canadians chanting in an exasperated unison while lying on the shivering floor in Heathrow Airport. "Give us fucking shovels and we'll shovel the runway, and we'll be in the sky in fifteen minutes."

You never actually realize how many people walk through the gates of an airport on any given day, because you never see them all at once. In security checkpoints, baggage claims, or departure gates, there are thousands at any given time. Because the lines keep moving, the magnitude of those numbers gets lost on you. The drunk, the poor, the rich, the famous, the happy, and the sad, they're all there, but over the course of the day they just become an anonymous wash of bodies.

At Heathrow that week, all of London—good and bad—was jammed into one cold place and told to stand still. Nobody was getting through those big automatic doors. The airport had become an insane asylum, the lunatics had seized control, and it was Christmas. Flickering lights advertised the duty frees and holiday discounts, and the airport bar was full of dishevelled men in Santa caps swiping worn and faded Mastercards. There was a hazy smell of booze in the air that in another time and place could've been easily mistaken for holiday cheer.

At one point I saw a junkie huddled on the floor, shaking without a fix. I'm sure his mom or dad had forked over the quid for the plane ticket. He was probably headed home for the holidays and had lined up a score at his destination, but here, trapped in Heathrow, he was helpless.

A toothless man scribbled frantically on a large sheet of paper as his caretaker nurse watched over him. Tiny little bottles of whiskey, empty, sat dead beside him. A drunk, red-faced English pub brute yelled in the face of an airline worker as she tried to calm him down. Parents with kids, all in tears, were everywhere, and crying babies, with the smell of shit from their dirty diapers, made the whole place stink while the bathroom lineups grew a thousand miles long. All around me, men with loose neckties were on the phone to their wives at home, screaming with panic and hysteria into the receiver. There was uproar. You couldn't even get nice and properly hammered, as the fear of passing out and missing your chance to board a plane overwhelmed you.

By December 23, some of us were herded like cattle into a tent outside, in the freezing cold, because the terminal had become too full and there weren't enough bathrooms for everybody. Reservoir was nowhere to be found, and Stagger, Billiards, and

Valentine had all gotten flights home. I was the only one left.

People were throwing up around me. Everyone had stayed up for days at a time in hopes of hearing their name called so they could catch a plane. Among us was an elderly couple heading off to see their kids for the holidays, and now this eighty-year-old woman and her husband shook with feverish cold, clutching stale cups of coffee underneath a thin sheet that had been given to them by the British Airways Authority. I was worried they both might die.

It was at that point that my name was called, and I was the last to be squeezed onto a plane to Canada that day. Running through the terminal, I never even looked back at all the people I was leaving behind. The plane took off through the cold grey English sky, and I waved a bitter goodbye to 2010.

When I finally got to my parents' house in Edmonton, my mom cried the minute I walked through the door. I'd lost about thirteen pounds and I hadn't yet told her about my teeth. With the rampant drug use and constant drinking, the sleepless nights, the weather and the misery, I probably had bags under my eyes that looked like they could hold snooker balls.

Despite it all, I kept thinking of Berlin, like a ringing bell resonating in the waves across the fields of Brandenburg, the North German Plain, and the Atlantic Ocean. The ominous might of the TV Tower, the liberating thinness of the Wall, the optimism in everybody's faces, the crowded midnight streets: it was like a dream that was still going on without me through every waking hour of every day. Because of all these things, Berlin seemed to rise like a phoenix from the fire of war, communism, and harsh cold winters, and through and over everything, I could hear the chanting: Berlin, Berlin, Berlin.

I spent the next year plotting my return as hundreds of Canadians and Americans all moved there in a mass exodus from North America. Moving to Berlin had become a kind of craze. I didn't want to jump on that train, though: I had in mind something infinitely more special, something that began at zero in all directions. I wanted to see Berlin like an artist, and not just someone who goes there with the hopes of being one, only to waste away their thoughts and dreams and ambitions in the back room of a dark German club. The answer was to tour and tour and tour.

A successful trip through Canada that took me to Victoria, B.C., and back to Toronto in about twenty-five days was the biggest focus of 2011, and, like a gargantuan itch in my brain, all I could think about was how much I wanted to return to Europe. Despite the catastrophe of the previous trip, I still loved the people, the audiences, the cities, the long, majestic ways the roads and trains seemed to stretch over the land like lines on an open palm. You could start to read these palms, I imagined, if you could just go there enough and become a part of the land and be invited into the geography, like the thousands of travelling musicians who had traversed its distances before you. If you could speak the language of the soil and breathe the air of the continent then it might just make you one of its own.

━╂┼╀╂╂╀┼╂╾

So there I was a few years later, on another long, long haul across the European continent. I'd started out in England opening for a Canadian songwriter named Julia Elaine, and we parted ways after two and a half weeks. She went across the channel to the Netherlands via Brussels for a few more weeks of shows alone.

Meanwhile, I headed east to Berlin to meet up with Wilfred Manifesto. We were to venture through East Germany, the former DDR, and play some shows in Poland and the Czech Republic, music dragging us by the ear across the continent. The earthly circumference of the railroad was about to carve crevices through our consciousness. These crevices are the memories that remain.

I remember being so thrilled to be back in Berlin.

I was climbing up the stairs to my friend Exene's apartment, and within me there was this strange feeling, like having a fist closed tight in your gut and stars in your eyes at the same time.

I had met Exene in a tavern in Toronto that was lit by candlelight, introduced myself, and, just like that, she said I could stay with her when I arrived. I was so taken by that. With nothing more than a handshake and a hello, we had gained each other's trust.

"Yeah, so call me when you're in Berlin in May, and you can stay with us for however long you want." It was February.

And she kept her promise. This was the first time I'd been back since Stagger, Jack, and I had stared up at the Berlin Wall, what seemed like years and years before. Since I was a stranger in Berlin again, not knowing anything about where to go and how to get there, she met me at the platform at Ostbahnhof and walked me back to her flat. It was there I first met her boyfriend, Aleksandr Rosenberg, and we all went out that night, getting typically Berlin-wasted.

We went to a small bar and slammed beers and talked about art. A *rauchen verboten* sign hung above Aleksandr's head that was only illuminated and made apparent to me when he lit a smoke. We argued and talked and laughed and howled like dogs amidst a pack of sheep, the hunger of an animal inside of us, thirsting to break the skin of the night. We talked about rock and roll and German techno, about the post-war world, and about painting and art and politics and the former DDR.

On a television screen hanging in the corner, there were images of flooding in the southeast German province of Lower Bavaria, in the town of Passau. Shots of German soldiers and locals hauling sandbags and piling them up to counter the downpour of rain continued for what seemed like five minutes. I watched the television out of the corner of my eye, kept talking to Aleksandr and Exene and the group we sat with, and then didn't think much more of it.

Drunk as shit, we left the bar and went to a club along the banks of the Spree by Warschauer Strasse U-Bahn station and got in the long line of people pissing in the river. I was feeling pretty wobbly now, and laughing in every language.

When we got into the club, the pounding rhythm of techno flew over my body like a cosmic wave. I ordered a Jäger and drank it fast, and as my blood started to pound, I threw up in the middle of the dance floor. In the next big wave I just kept dancing, as though nothing had even happened. I thought they'd be furious, but Exene and Aleksandr were keeled over, laughing hysterically, so much so that I thought it might be them who would hurl next.

We held each other up by the arms and spirits when we left the club under the full Berlin moon like wolves changing back to our human forms.

The next day was the only time, on that entire tour,

that I wasn't playing or travelling. I wandered around Berlin restlessly, like some kind of happy warrior who had made it through the final battle of a great war. I walked around Friedrichshain alone and crossed the Oberbaumbrücke into Kreuzberg, and by two o'clock in the afternoon I'd slammed a beer and the sun was reflecting off the Spree and through the envious green of my bottle. In silence I pondered the history of this place and stared back across the river at the East Side Gallery, that chunk of the Wall where I'd been with Stagger and Jack two years ago, and realized that it was the first time I'd ever been able to see it in the day, with all its makeup off, someone at their most honest and true, inarguably naked.

I wrote my girlfriend and tried to explain my state, but my language was slurred by a weary blur of alcohol and exhaustion. I thought of Exene and Aleksandr and dancing into the wild chasms of the night. I thought of the red wine and Jägermeister and how I'd soaked all of it up like it had become part of me. All of it would then flow through me, through my layers of skin, through the rubber of my shoes, down beneath my feet and into the soil of the earth, and hopefully a part of it would someday seep into the river Spree.

The next day, I had to leave once again, almost as quickly as I had come, and find my lonely way to Prague to finally meet up with Wilfred Manifesto for the tour's final run of shows. From Berlin, I was to catch a train via Dresden and to the mysteries of Eastern Europe. I overheard a conversation about the massive flash flooding in southeast Germany that now had made its way into the Czech Republic. I thought of that footage I'd seen in the tavern days before, of the German military throwing sandbags at the coming water. The barriers were up to ten feet high, enormous, and thick enough to stop a bullet.

On Czech trains, there are only private cabins, and you can pull the bottom of the seat out to form a bed that you can stretch out and lie on. If it's just you in the cabin, you can pull out every chair and transform the inside of your train to a full floor of cushions that you can write, record, eat, or drink on. I lay down beneath the window, the sun still shining in on me, and slept off the previous Berlin nights.

It was then that I first dreamt about my teeth. I was disoriented, falling, surrounded by a void of darkness. But this time, I couldn't feel myself swinging into the wall like I'd remembered. Instead, in mid-air, I reached out somehow with my bottom molars and bit my top two teeth out myself. Blood followed me downwards through the air and stained the skin around my mouth, and my teeth started chattering, chattering, chattering in a dark unison with the percussive train tracks that pounded along beneath me, chattering and chattering.

When I awoke, I couldn't tell if I was still in the

middle of it, that otherworldly and fantastic dream. The floods on the news were in reality far worse than I ever could have imagined. The cameramen collecting footage of soldiers amid the southeast German rain hadn't pointed the camera over the border at the sheer damaging horror the weather had inflicted on the countryside of the Czech Republic. To say that I awoke to what could have been mistaken as the end of the world would be an understatement. This was the eradication of entire ways of life—entire villages and towns and highways lay underwater.

The railroad between Berlin and Prague is elevated and runs above towns, which were barely visible on either side beneath the floodwater. On the left of me, towering highway road signs stood like tombstones of a lost civilization, and the tops of roofs of four- or five-storey apartment buildings looked equally as dead on the right. Rooftops were covered in salvaged goods that families would float up to in rowboats, continuing on like this for hours and hours, the train almost grinding to a halt countless times, the state of the railroad ahead uncertain. All that remained of cities was a faded dream.

On those boats, people would peer into dark windows to try to get a glimpse of what remained of their lives. In some cases cars drifted by like dead bodies and people in lawn chairs drank away their tears along the side of the tracks. Children and families, trying to make sense of it, just stared at the passing train as speechless passengers gazed out the window. It was like the Czech countryside had been swallowed by a gigantic and frightening beast, this thought itself exhausting, made nearly insurmountable by the fact that it took me almost nine hours to get to Prague instead of the usual five. The train crawled along, water inching ominously close to the edge of the rails the entire way.

I imagined some kind of spectre that haunted Europe, taking different forms throughout history: the Roman Empire, feudalism, the Black Plague, the Franco-Prussian War, World War II, fascism, and communism being this ghost at its most violent and oppressive. And now here it was again, poking its head through the soil and laughing at its own little practical joke. The spirit that had hounded the continent time and time again in the form of war and horror and disease also haunted on a much smaller scale, people caught within its hazy, foggy roar, and then it would just snap its fingers and return to its hibernation.

The train didn't speed up until it was closer to the city, which was also itself a watery mess. When I arrived in Prague, I discovered that the metro was closed because the underground stations were completely full of water. The Charles Bridge was closed too, because the Vltava was at record levels and inching closer to the bridge's underside, teasing all those stone statues of saints, standing without an audience or purpose. Maybe the haunting ghost of

Europe would swallow them too. I took a cab to the venue, far in Prague 6, and walked into the bar.

And there was Wilfred, sitting, scribbling in a notebook at the table. Bulky and hunched over, deep in focus, all set up and loaded in and soundchecked, prepared, calculated.

"Holy fuck," I yelled, a sweaty, barbaric sight, looking like I'd seen a ghost. "You won't believe the fucking day I had."

I ordered a beer from the bar. Slowly I felt myself become something real once more. The blood returned to my face and I didn't feel so pale. I tried to explain to Wilfred my last few weeks on the road: what began in London with Julia, and weaved its way through the Great German Plain to Berlin and then ended up here, at this table, ready to begin again.

The show was fine and we were escorted out of the bar to the band room, outside and across the street in an adjacent flat.

"There was a party here last night," the sound girl said to me, and unlocked the door. The putrid smell of sweat was like a steam hanging in the air. She opened the window, and Wilfred put his bag at the foot of the bed. The floor was covered in a carpet of empty bottles and broken glass. There was a closet with what looked like a few thousand dollars worth of vodka and tequila, all with names I couldn't read in Cyrillic, and a thin layer of black soil in the bed that was left in the opposite room. It had looked as though someone had taken a plant out of the flowerpot and shaken it by the leaves over the sheets. I put my bag at its foot, covered the dirt with a blanket from the bed beside it, and felt very far from home.

She said goodnight and shut the door. After she left, Wilfred looked up at me.

"Well," he said, "we're not staying in this shithole sober. Are you ready for a night out in Prague?" A few minutes later we hit the streetcar in Prague 6 and headed for Old Town.

"They used to have undercover officers who would sit on the tram and catch you if you didn't pay," Wilfred explained. "Once I was on the train here, and a guy who we thought was just a skateboarder stood up at the front of the streetcar and started checking tickets. Just one of those perfect examples of that weird paranoia-as-police relics of communism."

I took my chances and walked on. Nobody caught me. Normally we would've taken the metro, but the whole underground was still closed and submerged. By now the sun was down and the Vltava River looked even more menacing. A few blocks from Old Town we got out, went into a drink shop, and bought some fuel. I cracked my beer at the counter with an opener at the till.

Wilfred kept pointing at the architecture. "It looks like some kind of dream," he said, over and over.

And then curving around the corner after peering its eye at us for minutes undercover, maybe unbeknownst to me because I just wasn't exactly looking for it, came Old Town Square.

First, that spire. The big piece of black metal stretching upward, illuminated by the darkness of the night, seemed to have been encircled by an army of fallen angels with halos made of flies. And in that one moment, I believed in magic—the darkest, most brutal kind. Old Town Square at night when you're piss drunk is like a hand that reaches around the outside of your soul and squeezes all the liquid out.

A guy came up to us and tried to sell us weed and ecstasy and then offered to buy us each a shot of vodka for coming into the strip club that hires him to solicit out on the street. After two beers and a few rounds of shots we left, and walking back along the river we could see the spire rising again, becoming more and more violent. Wandering around, measuring the passing of time in hits of absinthe, dipping into a crowded bar full of obnoxious, drunken English kids on spring holiday, we caught a tram back to Prague 6 and I ventured into that room of uncorked liquor and poured a glass of tequila as Wilfred and I surrendered to the night.

The next day I came to on the train. I don't remember waking up in the morning—the tequila had robbed me of that. We were headed to Chemnitz, and for the second day in a row I bore witness to the destruction the floodwater had laid upon the citizens of the Czech Republic and the little that was left of their lives. I barely had the energy to go through another round of it, so I stretched out on the chair to sleep as Wilfred took photos from the window. "This is like hell on earth," he said, and better understood my day previous.

I awoke a half hour from Dresden and out of the flood. We were transferring to Chemnitz here, at the point of the day when the shadows are long and everything is a hazy yellow. At Dresden Hauptbahnhof we got out and killed an hour, walking along the main district of the town. I was now soaked in a deep sweat that clung to my clothes after leaping from my hair and skin, the kind of hangover that stays with you all throughout the day, inside your bones, up until you have your first drink. At that point, just waking up in the early evening, I was looking forward to the next time I could dive headfirst into the night and had replaced my pounding storm-drain headache with optimistic anticipation.

Chemnitz is like a postcard from the DDR, circa 1989. Windows the length of buildings have been replaced with sheets of plywood. No one has a job and the grass is overgrown. Throngs of kids, angry and frustrated, turn to the far-right of the political spectrum, shave their heads, wave a German flag, and blame Jews and immigrants for the fact that their hometown went to shit and everybody lost their livelihood.

The shadows stood long and flat in the Saxon sun and the streets were empty. We found the venue, located in a dingy basement tavern alongside the railway tracks, the door unlocked.

In Chemnitz, it's as tense as a clothesline. You can always feel a fight about to start. We overheard two people across a foosball table talking about an anarchist squat that had had violent confrontations with Nazis in the streets, sometimes involving showers of Molotov cocktails raining from top-storey windows, exploding and igniting as the *polizei* would rip around the corner and everything would scatter.

Later on that night, when Wilfred finished his set, a group of skinheads gathered around the PA. We were ending the show, and the crowd had doubled in size, their shaved domes reflecting the lights on the ceiling. They were thirsty and ravenous. Wilfred and I both felt very far from home, east of the Berlin Wall, in the dilapidated ruins of the former DDR.

As I was packing up my guitar and getting more nervous by the heartbeat, one of them walked over. He towered high above me, and seeing his giant hands I realized that I'd just be food for his fists.

"You better not be done," he said in broken English. His brow furrowed. "Tonight, all of us want to drink, and *rock*."

"Okay," I said, voice shaking. I didn't close the lid on my guitar case. "I'm not sure what else we can play, though."

He tightened his fist and leaned into us.

"Do you know . . . 'Hey Hey, My My'?" he asked.

Wilfred and I laughed.

"Of course we do," we said and launched into a set of fierce Neil Young covers, played probably six or so, as a circle of dancers formed around us and our two guitars, amplified to all hell's volumes in an underground German tavern bunker, the lights red with a nocturnal energy.

We were fending off the violence of drunken, raging skinheads with the only weapons we had: acoustic guitars and songs by Neil Young. We weren't sure how to stop, so we kept pulling them out, anything we knew. An uproar of orders and clinking glasses by the bar on the other side of the room was like a percussion section to our stripped down rock and roll.

"'Only Love Can Break Your Heart'?" Wilfred whispered as the skinheads cheered.

"'Powderfinger'?"

"'Fuckin' Up'?"

"'Campaigner'?"

"'Transformer Man'?"

Song after song we went on like this, singing till our throats and fingers were red, dripping with sweat and totally exhausted. Some of the more obviously angry and raging skinheads left the bar, and a cloud of tension exited with them. We'd dodged a bullet, or fists, rather, and there was an inarguable sense that the violence that had entered the place had been lifted by the spell of music. When we unplugged our cables and the bar's music came on, Wilfred and I looked at each other for a split second and let out a sigh of relief. We'd been playing for our lives.

"Come to the bar," someone shouted after we packed our guitars away. "We have to give you a Chemnitz tradition."

I went to the bar with Wilfred and there was a tray of shots waiting. I asked him what he thought it was, and we looked at the five clear glasses, pondering if it was gin, vodka, some rare kind of schnapps, or worse.

"*Prost*," I said to everyone and downed the booze.

My eyes shot right toward Wilfred, and I put my hands over my mouth, the putrid taste of whatever that liquor was racing down my spine, a feeling of blindness coming over my entire body. I ran to the bathroom, kicked open the door, and leapt into a stall, my whole head and body lurching over the toilet as I vomited.

"What the *fuck* was *that*?" I asked as I came out into the circle of laughing idiots. "That was the worst fucking thing I've ever drank in my life."

The bartender turned her back and picked up a twenty-sixer of clear liquor and proudly displayed it to everybody. Cloves of garlic were sinking to the bottom, circling and stewing in the half-full bottle. I imagined that it only got stronger as more and more bands came through, as more and more travellers were subjected to this brutal Chemnitz ritual.

"Thanks," I said sarcastically. "I guess."

Just like any other night on the road, Wilfred

Manifesto and I got piss drunk, maybe more so because of the fact that I'd just emptied the contents of my stomach into the bottom of a Chemnitz bathroom. We were taken to a small carpenter's workshop to be given hash by a burly Turk, and then upstairs to the bartender's house, where we passed out on an air mattress in the kitchen.

When we woke at noon, we realized that every single surface in the kitchen was covered in dirty dishes, to the point where it was as though the owner of this place had decided to just go out and replace the dishes he'd eaten on instead of washing the ones he already had. There were flies everywhere, feasting on the encrusted pasta sauce and various gravies and stagnant dishwater that were still filling up the bowls, and you could have written your name in the brown film on the walls. The top of the fridge, the floor by the door, the entire counter, the mountain in the sink—there was not a single place in this room unoccupied by stacks and stacks of dishes.

I got up from the bed, my head spinning in its usual morning ritual, and looked for the bathroom. When I found a towel I turned on the shower and realized that a showerhead was missing, so there was little more than a metal garden hose hanging from the tiles on the wall. Shocked I found a bar of soap sitting by the faucet, I made sure I locked the door.

When I got out of the shower, Wilfred was huddled on a corner of the mattress drinking a cup of coffee that the bartender had made for him as they talked about the night. He invited us for breakfast, and thank god we respectfully declined. Wilfred, looking around the room, was just as mesmerized and confused by the interior landscape as I'd been a few moments before.

I watched the bartender walk toward his front door, come back with a stack of yesterday's mail, open the letter on the very top, scan it for a few seconds, shrug, throw the whole stack on the floor, and walk away. The mail lay there, motionless and forgotten, just like the silverware and dishes that seemed to grow into a fortress around us. I wanted to go back into the shower and hide, my headache getting worse, but instead we got on the train as soon as possible, and went back to Berlin.

Our train pulled into Berlin Hauptbahnhof at six o'clock, and we stepped out under that massive archway of steel and glass and carried our things down to the U-Bahn. We were staying at an old Mitte squat called Schokoladen, which is one of the longest-running squats in Germany. Wilfred and I walked underground to Hauptbahnhof U-Bahn station and caught the train to Rosenthaler Platz via Alexander, emerged from the underground, walked to Ackerstrasse and into the bar.

Schokoladen was full of crust punks, anarchists, and a huge giant named Karl who took us downstairs and showed us the band room where we would spend our weekend. Six beds lined the floor, and there was a fridge full of food and beer. He told us to always close and lock the door so as not to let the cat in.

At around eight p.m. we got back on the U-Bahn and made our way to Neukölln for the show. Soundcheck, wait an hour, have a beer, play the show, get introduced to about ten people whose names you won't remember, go to the bar, get swept up by the light of the morning, repeat. Such is a tour. And so that's what we did.

After the show Wilfred introduced me to his friend Olli, a native West Berliner. He'd learned to speak English from watching MTV. He took us down the road to a pub where the hours stretched through the night and into the early morning's dull blue sky. There were beers and Jägermeister and a packed bar that only seemed to get busier as seven a.m. was approaching.

As the sun came up, Wilfred and I decided that it was time to go. Olli was drunk, and I was in that strange space where the light of the morning hits the yellow of your eyes and makes you wobble. I went into the *späti* to get a few beers for the train ride home, and when I came out, a group of people had arranged themselves around Olli and Wilfred. One person was rolling a spliff with one hand and holding a beer in the other.

I approached them and we all slurred some unimaginable mixture of German and English as the sun rose higher in the sky. As spontaneously as the morning itself, a man with an intifada scarf and no teeth emerged from an alleyway, ripped the joint from my mouth, placed his lips on mine, and kissed me in some kind of gesture of drunken kindness. He howled in laughter as I spat at my feet. All of the Germans in the circle were yelling something as Wilfred and I stepped back from the melee and I pulled my beer.

"That was gross," I said quietly.

The man sat down on a bench next to Olli, and I returned to the ring of smokers.

"Where the fuck did he come from?" Wilfred asked me.

"I'm thinking from somewhere other than a dentist's office," I answered.

We turned around once more, shocked to see Olli and the homeless man on the ground, enlaced in a drunken struggle. Neukölln's dirt was being kicked into the air as Olli lashed and jabbed at the guy. They both returned punches and blows and Wilfred was shouting Olli's name in disbelief. I took a drag of the spliff and looked around at everyone to try to figure out what to do.

And then, almost as quickly as it had started, they jumped to their feet and embraced like old friends. Wilfred looked at me with a raised eyebrow as if to see if it was the booze or the dope, or if it was really just Berlin bending reality. Two men had transformed from violently sworn enemies to welcome neighbours in a heartbeat. And with that, I finished my beer, bought two more, and descended into the U-Bahn. As we curved on the line approaching Alexanderplatz, I pulled Wilfred off the train and we ran out into the open square. The sun was high in the sky by now and there was a trumpeter singing the praise of angels, blasting out those golden notes into the first minutes of the day in the city, brass and yellow bouncing off the walls of the buildings that encircled us as they tunnelled through my ears and got buried in my dreams, dancing like ballerinas in and out of my drunken mind. We raised our arms into the air and ran like maniacs through the square. A man took our photograph as Wilfred danced and spiralled like a fairy possessed.

Arm in arm, we supported each other's weight and stormed back onto the train. Olli was long gone by then, evaporated like a ghost into the golden morning, and Wilfred and I were like two brothers in a maelstrom of rock and roll, holding each other up like a pair of ancient pillars. And then, still more Beck's.

We got to Rosenthaler Platz and slalomed around the drunks and junkies who were still emerging from their Mitte barstools and sleeping in the station. Coming out once again to the sunlight, we repeated our familiar walk to Ackerstrasse. When we got back to Schokoladen, we met a group surrounding a campfire that burned peacefully in the middle of the street.

Jesus, I thought. *When do you people sleep?*

The adjacent bar that was still serving brought us out more beers, and we exchanged linguistic differences before finally heading to the room and hiding from the sun.

What seemed like seconds passed, and then I awoke with the weight of a falling ton of bricks, as a sound rang out from upstairs. It pulled me from bed like a puppet. I went to the bar, my mind still in the boozy haze of the night and morning, and was met with a punishingly loud three-piece free jazz band from Warsaw playing at breakneck volume and making a pummelling racket to a full audience.

A bass player, a drummer, and a woodwind player, sometimes playing two instruments at once, launched themselves into a musical world dominated by sweaty confusion. They stared at and through each other, cueing with golden eyeballs, telepathically linked in sound: the noise got bigger and the band got sweatier, the woodwinds screamed and howled and the drummer was like one thousand waves beating angrily against a marble shore. The owner of the bar was the same man who'd brought us beers only hours before.

"You're back." He smiled. "Or did you never go away?"

I had to wake Wilfred so he could bear witness to the ferocious madness. This band was an angry whale exacting revenge on a wood harpoon. I ran downstairs.

"Wilfred—Wilfred." I shook him. "You'll never believe this. There's a show happening upstairs right now . . ."

When I convinced him to leave his bed and come back to the bar, his reaction was the same as mine, our pounding headaches forming perfect counter-melodies. Someone next to me lit a smoke, offered me a beer, and I didn't refuse.

"Did we even sleep?" Wilfred asked.

I couldn't answer.

Amid this cacophony, I knew that I was in a place where no time existed. I was a prisoner of my own chains, I had lived my life trapped by confines that only I had created. True freedom existed somewhere and at this point in my life, in Berlin, I was as close to it as I would ever be, or at least had ever been. All of this would fade to memory in seconds, but there was something that felt so violently everlasting in that big, circling noise.

All the while, the TV Tower hung in the sky like a hand grenade, a remnant of the peak of the power of the post-war east, a reminder to Berliners of their history and the strength it takes to stand together when divided.

━┼┼┼┼┼┼━

As you go further eastward from Alexander Platz, the front line of communism, you plunge deeper and deeper into a web of cultural, political, and economic recovery, and into Poland. I had taken the Berlin-Warszawa Express to Warsaw once before, but had never made my way down into the southeastern region of Silesia, the Polish heartland, its biggest cities Wrocław and Katowice.

The first thing you notice is how grey the skies get the moment you cross the border. Immediately things go dark. Anything east of Berlin is a thousand times cheaper than anything west of it, and a different rhythm—a fascinating rhythm—descends over the tracks as you go further east. So I'd always promised myself that I'd be heading back to that grey and overcast Polish sky, with all those broken windows in former factories that line the railroad and its rickety trains.

When Wilfred and I first arrived in Katowice following our tumultuous weekend in Berlin, we were taken to about four or five bars in the town square that were free for us as performers, and we were introduced to everyone who worked there.

"Later on," someone said, "we will have to drink some Polish vodka."

The promoter took us to the venue, a newly open and yet-unnamed art space in the middle of town, down the road from the cathedral. We sound-checked, had a drink, and planned our trip to Vienna the following day. After finishing our encore with the same run of Neil Young covers that had wound us all up in a frenzy in Chemnitz a few nights before, Wilfred and I dropped the bags off at the hotel room and went off in search of the real Katowice.

One thing you learn very quickly about drinking when you're on the road is that there are conversations you can have with people only at one in the morning, conversations that you would never have at noon. These conversations tap you right into the heart of a place. One interaction with a person who lives there can give you a glimpse into the nature of the stories of everyone's lives. Drunken, hazy, one-in-the-morning talk about art, politics, and culture transforms you from a patron of the bar to an angel of history, sacrificing the cells of your brain for a piece of someone's honest and uninhibited story.

Most often, you strike out, and all you get for trying is a pounding headache in the morning. But sometimes the alluring siren that is alcohol provides you with a golden experience, and it's the act of looking for gold that propels you deeper and deeper into the soothing darkness of the night.

With this in mind, as we were taken to a bar across the road from the venue, we were instructed by our Polish guide to "order the bus."

I told the bartender, across a few different language barriers, that that was what I wanted, and he went off to the back of the bar to retrieve the top piece from a tall stack of piled cardboard. I could feel a confused stare forming on my face, and as he unfolded the piece of cardboard to reveal five small holes, each about the width of a shot glass, I started to get an idea of what I was in for.

As he poured the five shots of vodka that I would be cheered on into drinking in under five minutes, I saw the outline of a school bus on the outside of the cardboard piece. He dropped the shot glasses full of vodka into the holes, and they sat there, motionless, waiting for me to drink them, like five tiny children on their way to class.

"Holy fuck," I said to myself, not sure if I'd said it aloud. I realized that I'd been drinking to the point of complete blackout intoxication for about six or seven nights straight, so by now there were holes the size of craters forming in my mind.

"And remember," someone said from somewhere around me, "when you order the bus, *you* have to drink it all."

Trying to fight off the hallucinations that come with holding off drinking during such a bender, the liquor pouring out of the pores in my pale skin, eyes probably yellow, beard long, voice broken, forehead damp, I didn't know whether to laugh or cry, but I drank them all and felt all those symptoms vanish as the last shot hit my bloodstream.

I imagined the vodka shots having little arms and book bags, yelling Polish children's songs, and cheering whenever the bus bounced. I imagined my mouth and throat and stomach as being the dark black cloud of adulthood that was going to instantly swallow all of that up, and I imagined the blackout that came after slamming the bus's five shots of vodka in under three minutes as being the death of an old, suffering man. From the cradle to the grave, all life, I imagined, came down to that dying second of intoxication and the darkness that followed. I started to become incredibly animated, like I was brought back to life. They brought us some great traditional Polish food and I started hugging and kissing everybody, the roof of my mouth tasting of boiled potatoes, beef tatarski, pickled herring, and lots of vodka. I gripped the glass of beer tightly and then things are really hazy after that. I'm sure there was some kind of deep conversation that occurred, but I'll never remember who it was with.

A faint green fog descended on the town square and I stumbled out the door of the bar and was met by the spire of a massive cathedral rising up over the haze, its bells ringing low. Wilfred shouted out at me and there was a hum of barroom laughter echoing off the brickwork of the road and buildings, and I fell down onto my knees, my guitar case smashing on the stones.

Morning came with the familiar feeling of weight. All the symptoms that the vodka had cured came rushing back to me once it had left my body. It's like all your thoughts are pained and clogged, and goop flows through your existence—the kind of viscous, molasses hangover where everything is slow. Then we got on the train and we went to Austria.

The next time I found myself in Katowice it was the fall of the same year. After the springtime tour with Wilfred Manifesto, I had gone home to see my parents in Edmonton to dry out. By the time the tour had ended, in Reykjavik, my drinking was completely out of control. I felt bloated and disgusting, unable to shake that feeling of pins and needles underneath my eyes. It had felt like the alcohol had made me just a memory of my former self, so I took a couple of weeks, shaking and sleepless in Alberta, to kick the liquor.

I returned to Toronto rejuvenated, sober, ready to start booking my next round of shows in Europe. I was healthy again and not depressed, and so not drinking as much either. Feeling optimistic, good about things. Up on life.

But on that tour I plunged back headfirst into the power of the road. There was always liquor in my bloodstream, I was an animal, a savage Canadian beast, exporting my life and thin blood to the world, running on the steam of a thousand broken engines.

When the promoter of the show and owner of the bar met me at Katowice station, she was looking and feeling under the weather.

"It was my birthday Friday," she said. "I've been drinking for three days. I have to take a night off."

I told her that I thought I would have to see it to believe it. She insisted though.

"Honestly," she said to me. "I think that if I drink tonight, I'm going to die."

It's the kind of statement that you can't really argue with and knowing how fucked up everyone seemed to get in this town, I decided she might be right. When I got to the venue, I met her husband.

"Heard that you had quite the weekend," I said to him.

"Yes, it was crazy," he said and laughed. "Constant partying. We're all taking the night off drinking."

I looked around and noticed that everyone was holding a beer.

"Probably a good thing," I said and ordered a Żywiec.

When I finished the set, I went to the bar to refill my glass. The promoter's husband was there, elbows rested on the wood, a mug of Lech or Tyskie filled right to the top.

"I was wondering if you wanted to try some good Polish vodka?" he asked me.

"I thought you weren't drinking?"

"This is just a taste," he said.

"Well," I replied, "in that case, of course." He poured two ounces of lemon vodka from a Silesian distillery whose name I couldn't pronounce, and we downed them both.

"Good, no?" he said.

Truth is, it was fucking delicious. I thanked him and started to walk back to the stage.

"Wait, wait," he said. "Want another?"

It was quite a lot of vodka for a night when you're not drinking, and he repeated this act probably another four or five times. I was back on that little Katowice school bus, with all those shots of vodka posing as children.

"Which one did you like the best?"

"Well," I said, thinking about the flurry of alcohol that had just stormed my way. Things seemed to be slowing down again—that murky, molasses feeling. "The lemon one, I suppose."

"Great," he said. "Me too. And the distillery is very well respected, very good friends of mine."

The vodka seemed not even to affect him. If this wasn't drinking, I started to wonder, what was?

We started talking about distance. I told him about growing up on the Prairies, about how in Edmonton the next possible show is three hours south or five hours east. "Bands do it all the time," I said. "But if you really want to get to the best shows of your tour, in Toronto or Montreal, it's a full four days of driving, of playing unpopulated prairie shitholes along the way."

"Wow," he said, his cheeks and nose blossoming into an alcoholic red. "Five hours from here, you're on the border of Belarus! Five more, you're in Minsk, and five more after that?" He paused. "Russia."

When you think of distance and time like that, once again you become trapped in a viscous substance, sliding slowly down the lid of the jar, and there's no escape. I thought about how far from Berlin I was, and about all the time and work it takes to get there when you've come from west of it. I thought about how much Europe there was still to come and discover when you cross it, an equal amount of Europe on either side. I had come so far, and still had so far to go. He talked to me a little longer about vodka, but I drifted in and out of attention thanks to the booze.

"Anyways," he said. "I must be off. Great night, great show."

"Yeah," I slurred. "See you later."

I realized this town was exactly the way I'd left it, in a green, blurry haze, shrouded in unreliable memories and late evening conversations in the burning hearth of the fire of vodka. Beneath its grey skies, inside those broken-window factories within those cities still technologically ten years behind, there are people who are so in love with the fact that you've made the effort to journey to them, so happy that you've shared all you have with them, and so gracious and kind that it warms you from the inside, warms your blood like the soothing heat of alcohol.

I was once told, after saying thank you to an audience after a show in a small town, "You say thank you to us, but really we should say thank you to you, because you bring with you a piece of everywhere you've been and so through you, we learn about the world."

History is geographic. You can feel it as your body moves great distances along the soil, along the railroad, toward or away from the sun, along an overflowing river or beside a gigantic mountain range. It is written on the ground in the movement or stasis of people, landlocked or spacious, imprisoned or emancipated by a body of water. The movement of ideas and the conquest of nations is determined by the nature and location of the rocks on which we stand.

The playing of folk music can be seen as a small addition to this canon. The peaceful sharing of stories and ideas, on a path carved by steel, through the rock, to end up in a new, manmade habitat, the city, the ultimate conclusion to the geographic effects of history. In Europe, folk music predates the arrival of industrial capitalism, stories and ideas moving freely across borders long before the printing press or spinning jenny. Touring in the modern sense—on a highway, with a guitar—doesn't predate capitalism in North America, so it's only ever been conceived of in that context on our soil. In Europe, people have been doing it forever, and to play folk music in the Old World is a chance to tap into that long, epic genealogy that stretches far past the beginning of borders and time.

The act of drinking with the folk you're playing to is a violent and unpredictable partner in crime to the music, the sidekick of the songs. You learn about a place over a bottle of beer, or wine, or vodka. Somehow, all the pain and headaches, all the anxiety and shaking and withdrawal that follow for so many mornings are all made worthwhile in those moments where you first talk with people in a place you've never been.

Was it the liquor or the act of drinking it with those people that I was addicted to? My body felt so much better when my lips returned to the taste of alcohol, and my words as sharp as the sword of a Teutonic Knight. But my mind was most at ease when I had someone there to share my words with. As soon as the darkness fell, I'd be ready to receive all the ideas and experiences that stampeded over the history and geography of wherever I was like a giant horse, that eventually entered the bar and charged around the tavern, angry and unbridled.

The train from Wrocław to Vienna heads south through the Moravian capital of Brno, in the eastern Czech Republic. At ten a.m. I boarded at Wrocław Główny, and after three stops an announcement in Czech blared over the loudspeakers. I asked the guy across from me if he spoke any English.

"Yes," he said, "it's some kind of delay. We're going to miss our train, so we'll have to figure out another way to Brno."

His name was Jan. "Are you a musician?" he asked me.

I told him what I was doing, trying to carve out enough cash to pay off a chunk of my MasterCard and maybe pay my rent, and do it by doing what I loved more than anything.

While checking the train schedules and connections on his computer, he remarked how strange it was that a Canadian would come so far east, beyond Prague and Berlin, into Silesia and Moravia.

We got off at this tiny border town called Ústí nad Orlicí, and the station was nothing but a wooden plank, a small ticket hall, and a café amongst thousands and thousands of miles of deep green pine. It was the furthest away from anything or anyone I've ever felt in Europe.

Jan laughed and joked, "We are going to disappear into the wild woods of the Czech Republic."

A man walked across the tracks, in front of a stopped train, and entered the main hall. Such a thing would land you a two thousand euro fine in Germany, but this was the closest thing I'd seen in ages to ravaged, untouched heartland, hours away from everything, so barely anyone noticed. Waiting for our connection, we went into the bar and ordered some food. I had a beer and Jan got this famous Czech liquor that tastes like a mixture of Jägermeister and flat Coca-Cola. Everyone stared at me, shocked to discover someone who didn't speak Czech. I knew then that I was deep within the heart of a country, the equivalent of being stranded in Brandon, Manitoba: rural Europe, the middle of the continent, a part of it I'd never seen.

That's the kind of experience that only the train can bring you—the railroad slices through terrain that highways can't.

On the highway, your life is defined by gas stations and rest stops, while the railroad injects you into the vein of a culture. You see into the backyards of houses when you arrive in a city. You hear the language all day and interact with other passengers. You end up at a rail town tavern, killing time between delays and sitting across from a group of Czech bikers and skinheads, the walls adorned with unfamiliar words, flags, and symbols, the air thick with an immeasurable amount of cigarette smoke and alcohol, the walls stained orange with human interaction. And there I was in the midst of it: the train had delivered me. Its beating heart of steel and coal had pulled me in.

The train is an office, bed, bar, studio, toilet, dining room, practice space, and a searing, bursting harbinger of energy. It sweeps you up and spits you out. It is unforgiving yet cradles you like a mother of metal and electricity. It speeds along at the tempo of a culture, its windows a View-Master displaying the harsh and honest nature of a place and those who live there. It often takes you where you don't want to be. Through its lens you see things that you don't necessarily always want to see. As though in the middle of a celestial sphere of god, you float above a city like an angel and land in the centre of a heavenly circle. You stretch your legs and write a song and drink a beer and let yourself become the train. Through its arteries you connect to the vibrant and all-consuming pulse of history. I took a sip and tasted the railroad.

Jan and I had long parted ways when I finally arrived in Vienna. He had turned left that evening, and I right, on the platform of a station in Brno. "Hope I'll see you soon?" he said to me. I knew that would never be.

Now the Austrian conductor looked at my ticket, and then at me, and I told him how long I'd been travelling.

"Since ten a.m.," I said, exhausted. There was a breath.

"*Wilkommen im Austria*," he replied and handed me back my rail pass.

I got off the railroad at Wien Meidling and immediately boarded the Vienna U-Bahn to Thaliastrasse, my body shaking with the anticipation of finally being able to get off the train and hit the stage, to see my old friends Esteban and Stanze and reunite myself with the city that seemed like the thread from which you weave a dream.

⸺╂╫╂╂╂╫╂⸺

There's a quality to Vienna that's not present anywhere else. It's fiercely unique to the place, but it's also incredibly hard to identify. There's a mix of high class and low culture in Vienna that's distinctly Viennese, a self-importance through rowdiness you might call it, the roughness of a German city with the palm trees and fast pace of Italy, a relaxed and laid-back charm, with buildings that are falling apart, and lepers begging in the subway. Lamborghinis circle the Gürtel in an almost Mediterranean, dim blue morning light, sex shops and neon and the gruff phonemes of the German language bouncing off the brick work and tarnishing its beauty in a self-becoming way.

In Vienna, at night, the *würstelstand* gives you the best glimpse into the true way of life of the Viennese. After leaving the bars, a parade of drunks makes its way to any number of kiosk restaurants with plastic tables out front, as the homeless and alcoholic sit and yell in the street, the lumbering thunder of the train shaking the ground as it throws itself across the city above and below.

Plates dripping with the grease of Käsekrainer and crusty Viennese buns are everywhere as the lineup grows and the crowd changes from the down-and-out to the well-to-do. You're surrounded by every kind of person, from all facets of Vienna's classes and cultures, all here, ordering beer and sausages at four thirty in the morning.

The lineup of young kids and old men and gorgeous women and working girls hungry after a night in the dark and smoky Viennese bars becomes more and more animated as people press closer and closer together, the man behind the counter opening a beer with one hand and pulling a sausage off the grill with the other, and he's smiling the whole time, moving back and forth between the tiny walls of his kiosk—a grand ballet. A distorted radio is blasting Austrian club music to the throng of people that grow in front of the *würstelstand*, and it's as though the bars and clubs have just moved out onto the street.

This is the Viennese version of an Edward Hopper painting: common people caught at their most vulnerable, all walks of life, unaware that they're being watched and glorified. The young and old and rich and poor and healthy and sick are joined in this awesome power. Anonymous faces enter and leave your view, and then at some point it all dies down and fades to calm, like *Nighthawks at the Diner*.

"Look at this," my friend Esteban said, a few rows back from the front of the line. A long deep crimson sausage is pulled off the grill and dropped on a toasted Viennese roll. Six tablespoons of diced onions and four different curry powders bury it completely before it's flanked by mustard and ketchup. "So dirty! So fucking filthy, greasy. I love it." The romance in all this mess isn't lost on me. The ground is covered in stained paper plates, tiny empty Jägermeister bottles, and discarded Gösser cans. The smoke of the grill ascends to the heavens and nightgoers queue at the till as though about to receive a holy sacrament. The tables arranged like an outdoor café in the dirt out front are full of people celebrating the stories they're about to tell. A gorgeous girl in a red dress drinks a plastic cup of an Italian red wine while linked to her lover's arm, and they're laughing amid the dust, grease, and garbage that's strewn across the ground. Cars race by on the Gürtel, laughing drunk brutes come and go from the doorway of Thaliastrasse U-Bahn station, and as we hear the hum of Vienna rise up in a soothing roar, Esteban and I both laugh and drink and know that amid all this trash and unhindered humanity is something beautiful that could only be birthed by the mother that is the tender warm hands of the night.

I thought back to when I first went to Vienna—I think I was with Wilfred. We'd met Esteban and Stanze at the show and they took us to the First District, and as I turned those corners and the Imperial Palace emerged from behind a wall of trees I felt like I was in heaven, or at least whatever I'd imagined heaven to look like. The walls all sparkling white, the buildings seemed to touch the sky, and the district seemed never-ending. Immaculate buildings towered above us as copper figures of history turned green in the presence of time. A feeling of liberation overcomes you. Bullets would pass right through you as you vanish transparent amid the marble weight of history.

The morning after the *würstelstand*, I woke up in Esteban's apartment and had to board a train to Graz. My hangovers were reaching epic proportions. It seemed like days and weeks of drinking were always compounded into one terrible, horrifying feeling upon waking. Usually by about four or five o'clock the feeling would be replaced by booze, but that day I knew something was different. This was a punishing, alienating fear of the world and everything in it. A chemical sense of self-doubt and -loathing thickened my blood. It's nothing real, but it feels so true at that moment when the night before is leaving your body and the withdrawal sets in.

That show in Graz was a turning point for me. On those days when your nerves just can't be calmed and there's nothing in the world that can save you from your mind, you secretly wish that no one comes to see you play. That thought is disgraceful. A dark, unadmitted secret, one that haunts your thoughts and makes you feel a guilt so great that you'd think you're not worthy of your own words and music.

When I got to the venue, this old Austrian tavern called Café Prost, the place was already rammed with people. I wanted to sit on the steps in front of the bar and cry. They were all about to see me at my very worst. I'd done this to myself, caught up like a pathetic victim in the hurricane of touring, of people and stories and nights out in cities, and it was steamrolling into my present now, like a crushing ton of steel.

I was introduced to probably ten people, the collective of promoters that put on the show, and did such a great job apparently, and immediately all their names entered and left my life as though through a revolving door. I thought I was going to lose my mind—I was so over my head in this maze, and everything seemed impossible.

How could I have let this happen? Why did I let the night take me by the hair and drag me through its gutters? How did I so foolishly become a servant to the rows of flashing lights, pulsing to the rhythm of celebration, neon, culture, and human life? I was a sucker for it all. It surrounded me with its waves and I always let myself get washed up on its dry, sandy morning shore.

I wanted to blame Vienna, but it kept circling back to me. I hated myself for that, all these people there to watch me, and all I could do was struggle, like they were medical students on a day trip to a hospital to study some sick patient. It took so much effort to play those songs and remember those words. I knew that I had to get this under control, or drinking was going to become me—I was powerless against it. This was beyond life on the road. I'd started to depend on the booze to cure me of my yesterday, and that wasn't working anymore.

After the show I thanked the promoters and collapsed in the backseat of the van that was my only ticket to a bed back at the sound guy's apartment. When we arrived I felt this pain in my side and my lungs felt heavy in my chest, rising and falling as I lay down on a mattress in a room down the hall. The sound guy was in a great mood, singing and pouring another drink in his kitchen, yet I was silent, feeling totally destroyed by the very thing that I'd tried so hard to create. I'd been chasing that fleeting and often unattainable moment in the darkness beneath the stars above that can teach you all you'd ever want to know about a place and the people in it, but other times just as easily leave you with nowhere to go and nothing to show for it.

I could hear him unwrapping the plastic on a tray of lox and I could smell the fishy odour. He cracked a beer and his phone rang, and I was sweating as the whole apartment filled with salmony carbonation and a language I didn't understand.

Lying there amid his yelling and laughing, shouting in his thick Austrian dialect, I'd let that feeling consume the very reason why I'd come to Europe in the first place, and it was devouring me like a beast. I'd always dreamed of living for the song, of being an artist and starving for a greater good, and that night I had turned my back on those desires in favour of a faint glowing buzz beneath the eyes and a powerful headache that would pickle over the course of the day. As my eyelids dropped like teary waterfalls, something deep inside me vowed to change.

Before he left, the sound man said, "You think Vienna is crazy, but you have never had a night out in Graz."

The door slammed shut behind him and the whole apartment went dark and silent. I had the dream again, of falling into a black and all-encompassing pit. Again, I reached up and over my top teeth with my bottom ones, and, magically and plier-like, yanked them from my mouth as the blood rained down my face and into the light of the morning.

―――――

Modern Germany is the bastard offspring of tyranny, and Berlin is its eldest, rebellious son—a teenager rising up against its overbearing father. Hitler and Stalin formed a fist around these people and they have sworn forever since to break free of it.

A transgendered crust punk sells used phone chargers from a shopping cart in the Mauerpark Market. An art school student does a line of speed and goes to the club on Sunday at noon. A photographer sits and watches the beggars bloom under a eucalyptus tree on Karl-Marx-Allee while the TV

Tower hangs overhead. The bars never close and people talk outside until the break of day. Someone plants a garden on their roof. Reggae blasts from a stereo on the U-Bahn while breakcore in the distance engages in peaceful musical combat. Two lovers kiss in the streetlights. You can smell the coffee in the morning as the light reflects off the beads of spray paint drying against a grey brick wall.

This is Berlin, a rebellious and optimistic kid spitting in the face of its tyrannical father. It is the sights and sounds and smells of freedom, engaging in a violent war against the past, and I think it is winning.

Berlin pays a unique form of reparations by giving everyone within its borders the right to be who and what they want. You can dance if you like, or not dance if you like, and you will be swept up by the same intoxicating and liberating rhythm. Have sex, play guitar, drink water, smoke dope, and do it all in the street if you so desire. This is how Berlin makes peace with the past and exacts its revenge on those who wronged it. It owns the future: celebration, music, and freedom, for now and forever.

Görlitzer Park swarms with newcomers to Germany trying to sell weed or speed. They've even assembled office chairs by the gate and hang out all day, calling to potential customers. A lady with a cart sells rice and curry from two old plastic paint buckets as hundreds of kids drink beer and smoke dope by the remains of the old Berlin subway.

Leaving Görlitzer Park, when you walk up Falckensteinstrasse toward the Oberbaumbrücke, you're along the main artery that connects all the boroughs of Neukölln, Kreuzberg, and Friedrichshain, and in twenty minutes you can pass through the heart of culture and music that has an energy that permeates the air like an expensive perfume. When you cross the bridge and come to Warschauer Strasse U-Bahn station there are cranes towering above the people, creating apartments and sky-rocketing the value of post-commie Berlin. Drummers and saxophonists play ecstatic symphonies. Punks panhandle outside a nightclub called Suicide and every direction is crawling with people absorbing the uncertainty of life in waves of sexual pleasure and mystery.

For all these reasons, it's never easy leaving Berlin. Exene used to put me up at her place for days and days on end. It was like her flat was a charity for the revolving door of artists who would crash on the floor. Once while I was staying there, Exene introduced me to a friend of hers on the U-Bahn who was on his way to meet a dealer to buy some speed. After my show, Exene and I had gone to a club and I got so wasted that she needed to take me home in a cab. I woke up in the morning, still drunk, and there was Exene's friend, coming down from the uppers, speechless, smoking alone in her kitchen, and staring at the wall.

Exene lived right on Warschauer Strasse, five minutes from the U-Bahn station, where all the drunks would pour out of the train like some mass exodus at every hour of the day on the weekend. Right on the border of Friedrichshain and Kreuzberg, it was a ten-minute walk to Ostbahnhof, which could connect you to the rest of the country, and when I took that walk to head out for a long run of shows, I was always left to reflect on the boozy haze that would define every trip I'd had to the city.

I'd climb the stairs to the train platform in this grave, familiar way, always thinking of my next, quickest way back. This feeling of loss and desire would always descend over me when I'd load my bag and guitar on the train and see Berlin disappear in the distance, as I was enveloped by the woods and country of Brandenburg. The city seemed always to vanish—not necessarily get smaller, but just dart behind a cloud of trees—and I was unsure if that made it easier or worse for me.

"Berlin is beautiful," Exene would say. "But it can break you, like it is riding on your back, and you are the horse."

I played with the idea of moving there so many times, but the idea just never became a reality. I thought of the endless partying and how it's impossible to escape it unless you have the will of a great bear and a liver of solid steel.

"All these people," Exene said once, "they move here with passion in their hearts. They all want to be artists, to be in love with life, to flourish, and then

Berlin possesses them. And then it's Monday morning and they're pale as ghosts and they feel terrible and they put on their Ray-Bans and a tight black dress and they lie to themselves about feeling better. They move here because they want to be connected to their identity, and then they lose themselves completely."

I never wanted that to happen to me. The thought of getting swallowed whole and shat out like that by a city, like you'd never even existed at all, was terrifying. To be food for it, faceless, used for its survival, its sustenance, such an insignificant part of its grand and infinite story that you just become forgotten in it, like a single cell in a massive body—that scared me. But is that fear or sound judgement?

And so I was always in this process of leaving and returning. A train seemed to be always slowing down or speeding up at Ostbahnhof. I saw the same views leave and enter my life so many times that I got accustomed to a feeling that was so tragic and unforgettable when I'd first experienced it. It wasn't the act of leaving and coming back that I'd gotten used to, just the feelings of sadness and excitement that came with it. Those emotions seemed familiar, but Berlin itself was always foreign.

Once, on that train ride out I was headed to Kassel to play my friend Fonzie McKnightingale's bar. Fonzie owned the place with this guy named Lutz who used to hold illegal underground shows in the art school there. They were legendary, incredible parties that, in true German fashion, ended far and deep into the light of morning. When Lutz graduated, I guess he took his parties with him. He bought an old tavern with Fonzie, and they called it the Weinberg Krug.

Fonzie was a songwriter who recorded under the name Mockingbird. He was kind of the pioneer of rough-and-tumble folk-punk touring in Europe, at least for Canadians. Like Old Bull Lee to my Sal Paradise, he was a veteran of the acoustic guitar path who'd managed to carve out a name and a living in Europe, like he'd been tattooed with a rusty guitar string and an ink made from German rainwater, ages and ages before the modern wave of North Americans trying to stake a claim in the "nouveau New World" of East Berlin and post-Bloc Europe.

Fonzie also passed on the first slew of contacts that got me to Europe and because of that I'd always work with the same group of people to get shows, those same people, like sand in the sunblock, who would sharply rub up against you in that big viscous, gelatinous matter that's life on the road.

So, direct from Ostbahnhof to the Weinberg Krug in Kassel, I unloaded the guitar, checked the system, and tested the room. And then I was at the bar, where they served genuine Czech absinthe. They weren't sure if they could serve it legally at the Krug, but they didn't necessarily give a fuck. We used to roll and spark whole joints in there, smoke them down to the filter, then bust up a ball of hash and roll another, well into the morning.

Once, I even got behind the bar and started serving. I threw my CDs across the place and even hit some young girl in the eye, and moments later bought her a shot of vodka as compensation, drank one with her right at the table, and then ended up in a cab back to Fonzie's living room floor, throwing up out the back window the whole way.

And so here I was, another night at the Weinberg Krug ahead of me, drinking with Fonzie McKnightingale, my Old Bull Lee, until the early morning. Fonzie and I always end up slinging words across the room in a drunken five a.m. stew. He told me that he'd just bought a castle well outside the city, in the middle of nowhere, beside a smaller town close by. He was brilliant in his ability to buy property and businesses with money that he'd made from touring. The concept floored me. Buying a bar, then a castle, and from nothing—from thin air, from music. He had some insight, I thought, so when he talked, I listened.

"What you have to do is go to the end of the S-Bahn line," Fonzie explained. "Drive half an hour or forty minutes from that, and there, that's where you find cheap shit."

I pondered the trip that Wilfred and I had taken to Poland and all the magnificent potential that goes with a place being so empty and barren.

"What about eastern Europe, why not move

there?" I said. "Think about what you can buy in Slovakia or Romania or Croatia for twenty grand?"

"Yeah," Fonzie laughed, "but then you have to *live* in Romania or Serbia or wherever. You're so far away from everything. It's not about east or west anymore. It's so far from the end of the Cold War that you should just forget about that east–west dichotomy. It's not just the fact that it exists east of Berlin that makes it cheap nowadays. Any city of over a million people is going to be expensive, because if there's a million people who want to buy into living there, then it's gotta be worth something to somebody. What we're going to see is a battle between the city and the country."

I thought about the new economic world, the cheapness of Poland, the former DDR, and really anywhere significantly east of Berlin, and how even though you might live in rural Germany you're still only a heartbeat away from the monstrous artery of the Deutsche Bahn. Germany was still worth it, and that's why people kept going there. I also wasn't alien to the irony of a DIY punk rocker being so dependent on a system he despised. In eastern Europe, for example, the farther away you are from western capitalism, the more disconnected you are from the railroad, the airports, the highways, and everything else you depend on to carve out a living.

"I can buy into a castle in rural Germany," Fonzie said. "And if I do that, I'm still connected. I can still take a car to the S-Bahn and get to the nearest Hauptbahnhof and that connects me to all of Europe. Romania? Serbia? Poland? There's still so much infrastructure waiting to be built there. The middle of nowhere is still the middle of nowhere, no matter how little it costs."

Germany was quickly becoming one big city, with the amount of green space between towns shrinking by the second, the urban sprawl of Berlin, Hamburg, Frankfurt, and Munich encompassing every piece of grass that someone was able or willing to buy. It would take too long, according to Fonzie, for that to happen east of here. Too slow for the impatient musician types who book their own tours and live on trains.

"I want this *now*," Fonzie said. "I want to be connected *now*, and I can still be as connected as I need to be in the German countryside. That's what everyone's going to want to gobble up next."

Real, new-style European capitalism, coming from the mouth of a DIY indie rocker: "Don't bother going east. You'd have to wait just as long for opportunity there as you would waiting for a booking agent. Or a publicist. Or anybody else that doesn't share your hands-to-the-wall, DIY approach to living and playing."

I thought of Eastern Europe, and the former Iron Curtain, how the light of the West was slowly creeping eastward. The euro and the dollar coming for it, ready to gnash their teeth against the people who lived there. The fall of communism was a new dawn for consumer capitalism and a million more mouths with credit cards and bank loans, eager as anyone to line their pockets with the fruits of the labour of someone else: the Baltic Tiger, the price of rent in Warsaw, Gucci outlets in Kiev, the colourful high-rise apartments of downtown Ljubljana, these images came to me all at once. It was coming for all of it, like a crazed bird of prey on the hunt, in the form of urban sprawl. East or west, it didn't matter.

"Nowhere is safe," I said, "is what you're saying."

"In a way, yeah," Fonzie said. He packed a bowl of dope and took a rip. "If you really want to outrun it, you have to head for the country. Leave the city. But the difference is that, in Germany, you're still kind of in the city because of how connected you are."

On tour, everywhere you go, everyone is always talking about rent. It's this commonality, this unfortunate standard of connectedness, whether you're in London, Paris, Madrid, Berlin, or Toronto. Through this underlying expression of resentment toward metropolitan human society, the murmurings of many languages become universally understandable:

"What do you pay? It used to be less?"

"Increased by how much?"

"That's criminal, you're going to have to move away from London/Paris/Madrid/Berlin/Toronto/_____."

The defining condition of our time will be one where urban rent everywhere gets too high and all the culture flees the city in a mass economic exodus. And any kind of unwelcome displacement from the place you love to live is exile. No one steps in to help you, everyone is on their own. The cities in eastern Europe are safe, at least for now. But the talons of capitalism are attached to a pair of beating wings on a gigantic bird of prey that is flying through the grey Polish sky faster and faster, at the speed of information—the speed by which cellular technology throws money through the air.

We're enslaved by it. All of us. Fonzie's solution is to head for the country and try to outrun it, but it will catch up to you. It's a semipermanent solution to an eternal problem. Evade imminent cultural destruction, at least for now. Carve out a little piece of land where you are the voice of its definitive artistic creation, pay less to live, and compete with fewer artists clawing and scraping toward the same vision. Leave the city. Prolong the day until your piece of the world is demolished and reconstructed in steel and fibreglass that scrape the sky.

"How much money do you have?" Fonzie asked. I snapped back to attention after a doped out and boozy freight train of thought barrelled down my track.

I laughed. "Nothing, absolutely nothing."

If it wasn't for touring, I'd probably have loads of money. I could've had a house somewhere by now, maybe not in Toronto, but somewhere close by, but I'm determined to do just this, to tour.

"Of course, man," he said and laughed too. "I understand. Keep in mind I'm twice your age. I toured for twenty years until I figured out how to live off it, and then I had to move here. If I still lived in Canada, I'd be in the same boat as you."

I always wonder how long this will last, how long I'll travel the world playing shows and hoping for a time when I can depend on it to make a living.

Who will hear me?

How much longer will this go on?

I pulled my beer.

"I had an agent who was super committed to my Mockingbird project," he says after another big hoot from his bowl. "And I guess that everything was hinging on whether or not I got this grant from the German government. Because when in the end I didn't get it, he stopped returning my emails and phone calls."

The thing that people don't understand about DIY and punk rock is that it's not like you pick the life-style—this lifestyle picks you. Nobody will book your tours for you, so you do it yourself. No one will give you the money to record your album, so you record it in your bedroom. No one will pay for your publicist, so you do your own mail-out and cold-call the papers. True punk rockers, the ones who see only the finish line, the ones who at any cost will find their music an audience, are all victims of circumstance and necessity. The situation always commands the art.

Fonzie and I went to the *nachtmarkt* across the street to get more beer. I'd finished mine, and the fridge was empty. We bought four. I drank three. No topic was off limits. Words flowed the way of the booze and smoke. We talked about Swedish death metal and Norwegian black metal, we talked about girls, we talked about castles across the German countryside, we talked about beating off on the road. Whether or not, when you fly loose in the train washroom, the person after you has the faintest idea of what you did in there. We both snickered like schoolboys in a changeroom.

"Berlin is beautiful," Fonzie said, when I talked about my morning, leaving Ostbahnhof only hours before. "Obviously. But it's the furthest thing from a good city for live music. No one cares about guitars there. It's all post-this and post-that. They want to feel the punishing bass of German techno, the rhythm of the dawn of the new urban world. Gabber parties, hardcore techno, that shit—that city has the rhythm of all that deep within its blood. They want to escape the country, so they're the ones making it so expensive."

Thinking of that electronic pulse, in all that talk of eastern Europe, all that booze, all that hash and weed, all that music, those yelling, smoking, drinking Germans, all of them filling the Krug with exuberance and charging the atmosphere in the bar with the copper rush of a battery, I became exhausted.

And then I was in the dark, on the floor, dreaming drunken dreams of Poland.

⊣╬╬╬╬╬╬╾

I woke up late and, sweating electric bullets, ran through the escalating archways of Berlin Hauptbahnhof and barely caught my train. I found a seat and put down my guitar, caught my breath, and began my first real descent into the former Eastern Bloc.

Poznań is the first stop on the Berlin-Warszawa Express, and opposite the platform is an abandoned factory. Every window is smashed. I had an amazing idea of where I was, but I still had no idea of where I was going.

Under that grey and ominous autumn sky I kept staring at this factory and thinking of how it had gotten so neglected. Every stone that broke those windows lay innocently on the ground before being picked up and hurled, at the speed of destiny, through those factory windows. Who would know how long they would lay motionless waiting for someone else to walk along and pick them up?

I arrived in Warsaw at eight p.m., and got in a taxi at Warsaw Centralna. When I went to pay the driver, I reached into my pockets to pull out ten euros and realize that I'd forgotten to convert my currency. In broken English he told me not to worry about it and shrugged it off.

"Wait," I said, "I'll find someone to change it, I'll be right back."

I hoped that body language would explain it all and I went into about seven shops looking for someone to help this guy. Everyone turned me away. I returned to find him still standing by his cab, in the middle of the street, smoking a cigarette, not a thread of anger sewn on his face, no ironstone waiting for me there.

"It's okay," he kept saying.

I handed him the euros, insisting he accept them. I thanked him and apologized and thought about how back home someone would've fought you over that. He just smoked, shrugged it off, and drove away. Later on, I'd find out how much better it worked out for him anyway—the złoty is probably twenty to one to the euro—and maybe he'd played me the whole time, but I still felt terrible.

I found the venue, which was this old underground cavern that looked like it could have been a bunker in the war. Warsaw was bombed so badly that maps of before and after look nothing alike. I ordered food from the kitchen and moments later the cook returned with a different dish than I'd requested.

"This is not what you ordered," he said. "But I think you'll like it better."

I ate it anyway.

In a few minutes, Michal, the owner of the bar, showed up and we did soundcheck. Not long after the people started pouring in. A young guy approached me at the merch booth and told me how he knew and loved my music. I tried to imagine how that music got there, through the internet, how so far from Canada it would be so hard to find the channels to hear it, but it had still arrived, and I realized how rare it might have been for Canadians to come there and play.

I drank some more and went to Michal's apartment. He told me that he was going to his girlfriend's for the night, and I was free to do what I wanted. His apartment was among ten or twelve identical looking buildings in a simple, dense old communist district. These buildings were "Stalin's gift to the Polish people," he said, in a deadpan and typically sarcastic eastern-European style.

Immediately what struck me was how small the place was—it was a shoebox. I imagined every single apartment looking exactly the same, and then I imagined it in the seventies, all those people scurrying like mice in their little boxes. And then there was the view: Warsaw stadium.

"Well," Michal said, "I go now. Enjoy yourself. Do what you like. Make yourself comfortable." I was alone.

God, I thought, *how long has it been since I slept in a bed?* I recalled the long line of floors and couches that lay in my waste. And a shower? But when I turned the water on it was shrieking cold. And it just seemed to get worse. After minutes of waiting, the water was eventually so bitterly freezing that it seemed to be at a boil. I saw that gigantic, glowing stadium in the distance and wondered if at night they turn off the hot water to power all those lights. I thought about heating water on the stove, but the kettle was so small it would have taken hours. I realized that everything in the place was either a smaller, more worn down or an archaic version of something I owned back home: his laptop, his kitchenware, his bed. Under the lights of the Warsaw stadium I surrendered to sleep.

Since I was flying to London to do some shows in England, Michal woke me up with a loud bang at ten a.m. He'd come home to take me downtown to catch the bus that gets you to Modlin Airport. We took the tram to the dead centre of Warsaw and he pointed out the Pałac Kultury i Nauki: "Another gift to the Polish from Josef Stalin."

We got off the tram and walked to a parking lot where there was a line of people standing at the door of a coach. I thanked him so much for the hospitality, and he thanked me for the show. The ride to the airport through the Polish countryside was characterized by more grey sky, and the airport itself was a four-gate shack in the middle of a farm field. I was flying Ryanair.

When I got to the gate and through security, the clerk began weighing people's bags. When it got to a family of four, also flying to London, a long conversation ended with one child bursting into tears. The mother argued more with the staff and then she burst into tears as well. Then she turned to a garbage can and began throwing out her clothes. In that flurry of disbelief and confusion in that tiny little airport, I thought I must have been in the middle of some strange Kafka novella.

"They are moving to England," a man explained. "The father is already there and has been working for months, saving money. Their bags have all their belongings but they're too big to fit on the plane because of Ryanair's baggage regulations. So now they have to throw everything away."

I nodded.

That was the first time I had heard about the English opening the borders to the eastern European workforce, but it wouldn't be the last. In some pubs it was all I would hear men talk about. When that family landed, I wondered if the cost of the clothes they had to buy would have exceeded the outrageous Ryanair baggage fee of two hundred and fifty euros.

As the plane took off, I thought of the Warsaw cabbie who shrugged off my inability to pay him in his own money, and the cook who ignored my order. I thought of the casual hospitality of Michal giving his entire flat to a complete stranger for the night. I thought of all those Polish music fans in that underground Warsaw cavern. I thought of how someone could live in such an apartment the size of a small Parisian closet with no hot water after ten p.m., I thought about his empty fridge and his computer from 2003 and how everything he owned was just a broken or outdated version of what was cutting edge in Canada. I thought of that tiny grey airport in the middle of nowhere, and of what had become of that family, and of that run-down Poznań factory. And with all of those thoughts, I woke with a pounding in my head, and teeth, on the floor of Fonzie's apartment.

Between tours, I'd pick up some under-the-table carpentry work. One of the jobs was a bit-by-bit renovation that we could only do one or two days a week, and in total secrecy, since the owner didn't have a permit.

Toward the end of a long two-month stretch of irregular work, and on the eve of another tour, I was sistering a joist on the main floor while another tradesman tiled the bathroom upstairs. He'd gone outside to have a smoke and I followed to get a break from the thick cloud of dust settling on the hardwood floor.

We had to navigate around furniture, around bicycles, around kitchen utensils and pots and pans that were covered in tarps so as not to be cemented with the dust that was thick in the air. Of course, we started talking about work.

"I have huge bills to pay," the guy boasted. "Gotta work every day. Have to clear at least seven grand a month—seven *grand*—otherwise I'm totally fucked. Got my vehicle, some employees, I got my little girl . . ."

I told him I was a musician, on my way back to Europe, yet again, for another round of shows.

"You make any money doing that?" he asked me.

"Well, it depends . . ." I trailed off. "No, not really, I guess."

He finished his smoke, put it out, and leaned on his arms against the railing that circled around the back porch.

"Why would you do it, then?" He was smirking. "The fuck is the point?"

I looked at him for just a moment, pausing, trying to figure out what to say. I put my arm up in front of my eyes to block them from the sun. "Isn't that kind of like me asking you why you'd want to raise your little girl?"

We walked up the few steps and opened the door to go back into the house.

"There isn't a lot of money in having a kid either," I said, under my breath. "At least that's what I hear."

He wished me luck on the tour as I left for the day, and I went home to pack my bags.

A few weeks later, on the train crossing the border from Görlitz to Wrocław, I once again experienced the sudden change from the polished and clean architecture of Germany to being surrounded by buildings that were falling apart. The sky plunges immediately into a thick grey. Eventually the signs become an even more lifeless blue, and all the windows you see are broken. After you cross the border, the geography changes into the most remote and uncomforting aspects of the former DDR.

A man has his head out the window of an old communist shoebox apartment and he's drinking vodka at eleven a.m., watching black birds fly through the cold Polish sky. Children play soccer on a country field—but there are absolutely no houses around them in any direction. Rows and rows of decrepit garages line the railway on the outskirts of towns. The train I'm on is one lonely car. Passengers gaze forward through the open door of the cab and the front window of the train. I'm the only one staring out the side, at the grey Polish landscape.

A dirt road about six metres wide, with puddles as big as baseball diamonds, shoots off across a green and yellow farm field. And in the middle of the road, directly in the centre of it, is an old Polish lady. She's clutching a tiny plastic bag and walking toward the horizon. There's nothing but green fields around her, not a house or building for miles. Head down, through the puddles, shoes covered in the sandy, rainy muck, she carries on. After just that one glimpse, she begins receding. She gets smaller and smaller; but so do I.

I imagine she's never left Poland. That woman in her eighties, still following the road home, through all kinds of tyranny. Unimaginable to a Canadian mind, steadily on her journey goes. Maybe she once touched Josef Stalin's hand? As a little girl, perhaps she saw the tanks and red parades and lost her siblings and moved from the towering stacks of the city to a farm out here, closer to the German border, to escape it all ... And then the Wall fell, so she could have gone west, but she stayed. And here she is still, walking along a dirt path, to wherever it is she's always been going all these years, without even the faintest or distant idea that I saw her, walking to the edge of the horizon, as though about to fall off the edge of land, into the sky.

After the show in Wrocław, my second last before returning to Berlin and flying home, I sat down next to a man named Bartek at a table helmed by the promoter and drank a beer and talked.

"I find it amazing that you come around here," he said.

"Well, I love Poland. And it's not that out of the way from my German dates."

He laughed and said, "Maybe by Canadian standards."

Bartek had grown up here, in Wrocław, or at least somewhere close by. Everywhere I go in the former Eastern Bloc, I try to get someone to paint an image for me of what it was like to live under communism.

I just can't imagine how it really was. It's like imagining yourself as someone else: impossible.

"You will never be able to imagine," Bartek said. "And you shouldn't, it's not your job."

Then I asked him for a story.

I'd heard earlier from someone else on this trip that Czechoslovakia was surprisingly more liberal, that you could buy Jimi Hendrix records there, or other American music—that it was easier to be connected to art there than in other places behind the Iron Curtain.

"When I was seventeen, in the early nineties, I heard that Guns N' Roses was playing in Prague." He slammed a glass of wine. "And since I was leaving Poland, I had to go through all these ministries to get my passport. Days and days I spent, getting the paperwork together and filling it out. As a seventeen-year-old kid, all I wanted in the world was to see Guns N' Roses. Two days before I had to leave, when I finally had everything in order—all my paperwork, train tickets and concert tickets booked and purchased—I went to the police station to get my passport, and I was . . ."

Bartek paused.

". . . refused. I was heartbroken."

He talked of the EU and the euro and how glad he was that he'd outlived all that had come before it. I told him how critical some of my generation was and how disgusted some Europeans were that western-style capitalism had finally broken down its continental borders. He talked of how long Poland had tried to be involved. And at that moment, someone came by with a plate of cheese for the whole table, refilled Bartek's wine, dropped some chicken wings in front of us, and got me another beer. We thanked her, I thanked the promoter, thanked everyone, and Bartek continued.

"You see?" he said. "That would never have happened to me when I was growing up." He gestured at the food and wine that had just arrived. "All these young people take all that for granted. There was no such thing as chicken wings for a Polish person in 1988. I remember my mother taking me to the store and her handing over food vouchers and us getting two pounds of meat for the next however-many days. That was all anyone was allowed to have—and if they were out of food, then you starved, or had to buy it or beg from someone who did have it. Today I think about the people who worked there, who were obviously secretly taking more for themselves, who would've been left in jail to rot if they were ever caught stealing state property."

I imagined a Poland with an even greyer sky, with even more busted-up and run-down vehicles. With even more graffiti covering the buildings. With even more chewed up sidewalks and skinny babies.

"And that's why I laugh when people always talk shit about the EU in Poland," Bartek said. "We don't see what our other option is. We have a genetic mistrust of Russia. In my opinion, it is either align yourself to the west or the east—and the east has killed and murdered and imprisoned us for decades. The Russians have this idea that they were our liberators. They are shocked when we try to create a distance between us politically. They claim that they liberated us from the Nazis, when all they did was create a different prison."

Bartek told me the story of the invasion of Poland, about how the Nazis marched to Warsaw and flattened it, so not a single building remained. And on the other border, the Bolsheviks rounded up thirty thousand Polish intellectuals, executed them, and burned them in a mass grave, a mountain of human death.

"That was the Russians that did that to us," Bartek said, his outstretched finger pointing at the air. "And they say that it's western propaganda that tells the Polish otherwise. But we were there. All that we could know is the truth."

Bartek drank another glass of wine in one go.

"Fuck," he said, "I have to work at nine tomorrow." And then he poured himself another glass and carried on. "For me, as part of the older generation, the EU represents a chance for us to be free of fighting in Europe. For thousands of years there has been war in Europe. European history has been defined by the fighting of war on European soil. It is all we have ever known. The last century was so tragic that everybody had no choice but to admit that this finally needed to end."

I asked him about how much Russia had changed, if at all—about how different it is to write about or speak up against the government now.

"Now, in Russia," Bartek said, his words starting to quiver, "if you go on the internet and post something about the government, maybe a friend comes up to you and puts his hand on your shoulder and quietly says, 'I think you'd better leave.' If you stay, then a few days later, some mysterious men will come to the door of wherever you're staying and order you to go."

Bartek remarked how that was the only place like that in Europe now, how the war had slowly been won, that there were so many holes in the communist system that it was like a sieve made of paper that culture just dripped through and tore to bits.

"I am not right wing," he continued intently. "But for me, the EU was such a relief. The terror and sadness from when I was younger has been replaced by all this." He gestured at the chicken bones and empty glasses at the table, the discarded toothpicks we used to poke and stab at the bits of cheese. "For so long, Poland was something else. Not a normal place. And now, finally, after all that struggle, after generations of being conquered and controlled by someone else, we can finally be something."

The next day, I caught a bus back to Berlin, last night's conversation still playing out in my mind, as though it had happened moments ago. I met up with Exene and Aleksandr and we went to Friedrichstrasse, crossed Checkpoint Charlie, and jumped over that brick line dividing the former cities of West and East Berlin.

"So, reunification day must just be a huge party here?" I asked, echoing Bartek.

Aleksandr, a native east Berliner, born and raised in Lichtenberg, laughed. "Yeah," he said, looking back at me from a few steps ahead. "But for us East Germans, November third is a sad, sad day. That is the day when all the capitalists came and invaded our country."

I looked at the old military booth, and at the picture of the East German soldier with his medals of honour, the DDR hammer and sickle, and his robotic, communist smile, and then I looked up at all the neon lights and high-rises that line Friedrichstrasse, the Nike and McDonald's logos that hang like national flags and political slogans and political identities and propaganda commanding you to spend your money and adopt the ideology of greed.

At the former crossroads of East and West, these electric banners of victory stand tall and proud over the sidewalk and the countless food and liquor vendors that salivate at the sound of jangling euros in the pockets of passersby and the smacking of the lips of hungry American tourists. It seemed to me Berlin could never be unoccupied.

That night I was playing my last show of the tour. A few days later I would catch another plane, watch Berlin vanish in the distance, and return home to Toronto—where once again all of this would fade into memory. I loaded up my guitar to the venue, unpacked it, soundchecked, measured a few hours in pints, played the show, and went to meet up with Exene and Aleksandr at a club in Mitte.

I was done. Another tour finished—a month of life that seemed to race by in twenty minutes. You blink, rub your eyes, clear your throat, think about the ground you've covered, about how long you've been gone, and about how fast it all seemed to happen to you once you struck that final chord. All you want to do is get offstage and go home, but something in you, a longing, also pulls you back. You know you could find the energy to play another thirty shows, if only you had to.

When I found Exene and Aleksandr at the club, I was met with the usual pulse of German techno, so powerful and loud that it could alter your heartbeat. A huge crowd was pounding its collective feet against the hardwood at the front of the stage. I headed straight for the bar and bought a round and slammed it. And then I did it again. Vodka shots. And again.

And then we started dancing, in a big group holler, shouting at the top of our lungs. It was reminiscent of the time we spent at that club by the Spree years earlier: time stood still in that moment, frozen in the heat, and then passed, like exhaling lungs after a drag on a cigarette. There we were, flecks of sand in the suncreen.

They kept dancing, but I stopped to take it all in: all that had happened, all that was to happen, and all that could have happened. Berlin rubbed its sweaty body against me and I kept going back to the bar, as to an altar.

Aleksandr was a rickshaw driver and had to work the next morning, biking American tourists around the city, pointing out landmarks and destinations. They'd ask where they could find the best schnitzel, the best burger, tip him well, talk shit about the Democrats, spend their money on the city. Aleksandr laughed about it because in his eyes each one was as stupid as the next. But it was great money.

So we disappeared into the night, drunkenly stumbling, and Exene stayed behind to keep dancing with her friends. In about three minutes we came upon another *späti* and I convinced Aleksandr to have another beer and shot of vodka for the U-Bahn ride home.

I came to on the platform of a subway station and wondered what time it was. I had a faint drunken memory of leaving Aleksandr on the train and getting out at what I thought was my stop, but apparently I'd gotten lost. Confused, and as the hours crept by into morning, I must have submitted to my exhaustion and sat down on the platform again and closed my eyes.

I was awoken by the prodding of two policemen who picked me up and escorted me out to the street and then to a bright public square.

"I'm so sorry," I kept saying. "I'm so sorry, I just want to go home . . ."

They kept assuring me that it was fine, that I wasn't in trouble, that they just wanted to get me out of there so I wouldn't get robbed, or worse. That it was safer on the street, in the dim morning light, than it was in the tunnelling underground of the U-Bahn. I thanked them, rubbed my eyes a little, tried to channel the dark recesses of my unconscious sober brain, and somehow made my way back to Exene's apartment.

When I woke again that afternoon, Aleksandr was upright in bed, his hand over his eyes in shame and fear. His work kept calling, wondering where he was. Exene had her hand on his shoulder, and his shirt was off.

"What happened last night?" I asked.

"Someone stole my wallet and my phone," he said. "I had them in a bag, under my shirt, under my jacket. Someone unzipped my coat, lifted up my shirt, opened my bag, and saw my wallet—and a phone that cost me three hundred euros. They took them both, and I was so drunk I didn't notice."

I moved my tongue around in my mouth, pressing it against the spot where my teeth used to be. *What, I thought, I would've given to have woken up that morning, years ago, missing only a wallet and a phone.*

The room went silent for a second. "Jesus," I said to him. "I'm so fucking sorry, man."

As the day went on, I killed more time, went to flea markets, kicked my hangover in the ass, drank water, and avoided the bar. The next day I flew home to Toronto, thinking of how Berlin defeats even the most hardened Berliners. It is beautiful, but it can also break you, I remembered Exene saying.

On the plane home, I had another dream. For once it wasn't the one where I bit out my own teeth. It was a much quieter, better dream.

I was on a train, alone, under a vast and overcast sky at dusk. The night was beginning to wrap itself across the horizon like a giant blanket, and the train tracks were cutting through an enormous field. In the distance I could see tiny, unlit buildings, maybe farmhouses, like little black shoeboxes. I had no idea how I got there. I didn't even know what my last memory was. I didn't know where I was going, and I had the feeling that it might not necessarily be somewhere good. I was just going where the rails were heading.

Someone had to be conducting the train. Someone had to be sitting at the controls, guiding it to where it's supposed to go. But I was never going to meet the person taking me on this journey, because they were four or five train cars away, and the cockpit door was closed.

When I awoke, I landed at Pearson Airport, and I took the bus home.